Light in the Crossing

ALSO BY KENT MEYERS

The River Warren
The Witness of Combines

Light in the Crossing

STORIES

KENT MEYERS

ST. MARTIN'S PRESS ❋ NEW YORK

LIGHT IN THE CROSSING. Copyright © 1999 by Kent Meyers. All rights reserved. Printed in the United States of America. No part of this book may be used or reproduced in any manner whatsoever without written permission except in the case of brief quotations embodied in critical articles or reviews. For information, address St. Martin's Press, LLC, 175 Fifth Avenue, New York, N.Y. 10010.

Grateful acknowledgment is made to the following publications in which these stories first appeared:

Crazyhorse, "Two Speed"; *The Georgia Review*, "Easter Dresses," and "Light in the Crossing"; *The Ohio Journal*, "The Husker Tender"; *New England Review/Bread Loaf Quarterly*, "A Strange Brown Fruit"; *The Sonora Review*, "The Heart of the Sky" and "Wind Rower"; *The Southern Humanities Review*, "Making the News"; *Crosscurrents*, "Glacierland"; *The Minnesota Monthly*, "Bird Shadows." Portions of "Two Speed" were published in a different version in *The River Warren* by Hungry Mind Press. Used by Permission.

Library of Congress Cataloging-in-Publication Data

Meyers, Kent.
    Light in the crossing : stories / Kent Meyers.—1st ed.
        p.   cm.
        Contents: Two-speed—Easter dresses—The husker tender—Light in the crossing—A strange brown fruit—The heart of the sky—Wind rower — Making the news—Glacierland—The smell of deer — Abiding by law — Bird shadows.
    ISBN 0-312-20337-3
    1. Minnesota—Social life and customs Fiction.   2. Country life—Minnesota—Fiction.   3. Farm life—Minnesota—Fiction.   Family—Minnesota—Fiction.   I. Title.
PS3563.E93L54   1999
813'.54—dc21   99-22069
                                                                CIP

Book design by Ellen R. Sasahara

First Edition: August 1999

10   9   8   7   6   5   4   3   2   1

To Wendy and Tom

Contents

Acknowledgments

Many people read one or more of these stories and gave me helpful advice, most significantly Wendy Mendoza, Tom Herbeck, and Al Masarik, but also Denton Ketels, Sue Morrell, Scott Cawelti, and Stewart Bellman. My editor, Carrie McGinnis, recognized and shaped the book with her acute understanding of its center.

Noah Lukeman, my agent, has been a constant source of encouragement. The editors and staff of all the journals where these stories first appeared sustained me. Most of all, my wife, Zindie, quietly and constantly, for years, has advised, encouraged, sustained me.

Light in the Crossing

Two-Speed

I went to Two-Speed Crandall's funeral not because I had any affection for the man, but because it's the kind of thing you do around here; you show if not in life, then at least in death, that the people whom you have talked about and nod-ded to, who have occupied a spot of ground close to your own for the years of your breathing and eating—you show that they were, after all, part of your community. Two-Speed Crandall, as far as I can see, gave nothing to this town worth having—and I've thought hard about this, and I'm trying to be fair, and I have no grudge against the man. I didn't go to his funeral to mourn him; I don't intend to miss him. But I didn't go to celebrate his dying either, and that, it seems to me, is as impartial as I need to be to fairly make a claim to it.

Two-Speed's family consisted of his wife, LouAnn, a woman hardly ever seen, and their three sons, Matthew, Mark, and Luke—names, I've thought since I was old enough to think such things, poignant enough to be painful, speaking certainly of LouAnn's, not Two-Speed's, dreams for their children, and as un-prophetic as names could be, since the boys had neither religious nor literary leanings—in fact, quite the opposite, Matt and Mark celebrating their sixteenth birthdays by staying away from school and never returning, and Luke, though finishing school, returning to Cloten to spend his nights catfishing on the river.

The boys boasted of their badness whenever they could, but in truth, they were nothing but small-town bad boys, their badness constrained by the same smallness they pretended to escape from with it, limited as much by their possibilities as by their imaginations: stealing candy from the grocery store when they were younger, throwing green apples at the sheriff's car as he did his daily patrol, setting fire to an abandoned barn in the country, which blazed like a torch on the horizon—everybody in Cloten, awakened by the fire sirens, standing on their lawns watching it, while the fire trucks sped out of town, and the knowledge of who had set the fire, though never proven, passed from lawn to lawn through the whole town before the sound of the sirens, coming back across the flat fields, had faded into the night.

These activities of Two-Speed's sons—as well as the way they flunked their classes not out of stupidity but through sheer stubbornness—were frowned upon but tolerated. But when Matthew, the oldest, came to school with a cattle prod and shocked several of the school outcasts with it—the clumsy and stringy-haired ones who were the butt of jokes by nearly everyone, forcing from their throats and chests sounds like pieces of raw meat being slapped together—the students rose in a wave of outrage that overwhelmed and subdued even the Crandall brothers, the students having seen, most of them, what a cattle prod could do, how its blue, sizzling arc jolted the slowest and dullest steer, thick in its flesh, into a snorting, slobbering, and panic-stricken lunge up the chute and onto the truck.

The stories went around for a long time afterward of how three of the football players—some said upon the advice of their coach—confronted Matthew behind the band saw in the shop and took the cattle prod from him, which he had stuffed down inside his boot and up along his leg, and they smashed and bent it and finally sawed it in half, and all the while, the stories a dozen times removed by the time they came to me, said that Matthew looked like he would weep, that he turned white and as still as cast aluminum, and stared in silence, only his lip trembling a little, as the saw whined through the prod.

For a long time the school laughed at this comeuppance, the tough and nasty one having his toy taken away. But when I asked my father about this—I was twelve at the time and thought he would rejoice in the story, and I told it to him after school with the mild euphoria of knowing I would please him—he only stopped working and looked out across the tangled cornstalks left by the combine.

"Don't you think it served him right?" I urged.

Still he said nothing. I felt my smile of expectation solidify on my face. Then I became defensive. "Everybody's laughing about it," I said, squinting.

He reached out and put one hand on the lugs of the tractor tire, then leaned his whole body into his shoulder. He looked down at the ground, then up again. His expression was so distant and turned inward that I thought he might not have heard me.

"Yeah, well," he finally said. "It was probably Two-Speed's prod."

"So?" I said.

He leaned his back against the tire, took off his gloves, beat them down once against his thigh. The leather smacked, and dust discolored the air. My father had pale eyes, and when he raised them to the horizon again, they were even paler than I knew them, and he kept them fastened out there when he spoke, to where the fall sky was almost white.

"There are a lot of unpleasant people in this world," he said. "Two-Speed's one of them."

Two-Speed drove semi for Niebuhr's Trucking and often hauled cattle for us. "He spits," I said. "He swears a lot."

"He beats his kids," my father said. He looked down at me and caught my eyes. It was like something from the way-off sky had come into his. He hit his gloves against his pants leg again. "Do you think Matthew figured out how to use a cattle prod that way all by himself?"

Leaning as he was, my father was barely taller than I was, and we looked right at each other, and this was the first time he'd ever talked to me this way, about something so serious, as one adult to another. I hardly comprehended it. "You mean?"

I couldn't take my eyes off his face. I searched there for some clue as to how I ought to feel.

My father nodded, his mouth tight. "That's what I mean."

Since then I've come to know that Dad's opinion had

support in rumors both direct and indirect, and in the famous nastiness of Two-Speed's threats, when leaving the bar late, to have it out upon his worthless sons. If all this is true, Matt certainly had reason to tremble, his blood reason to flee his face, upon the realization that his stealing of the cattle prod would in due course be discovered by Two-Speed and an appropriate and punishing justice exacted with some other implement equal to the task.

Of course it was all rumor and talk. Even if it had been proven, probably nothing would have been done. Family matters, in those days in a town like Cloten, had an aura of the sacred. Nevertheless, I mark that conversation with my father as my introduction to adulthood and the dark secrets that reside there. So now Two-Speed's death turns me back to think of him again, and to feel an old attraction made safe, perhaps, by his passing.

He was a man who lived on the bare edge of our community, yet more stories were told of him than of anyone else in town. Two-Speed was tolerated when he was working but otherwise avoided during the day, but at night he entered the uneasy camaraderie of the bar, earned, even, a kind of grudging respect there for his willingness to fly into a fighting rage over anything and with anybody, and for his unfeigned refusal to glance at a clock, ever, or to find familial reasons to leave.

As a worker, he had the one great advantage that he was always available, without contravening obligations, though he was not always willing or sober, and he possessed—his greatest source of pride—a Class A driver's license. This license, the stories say, he always produced at some point along the downward slope to drunkenness, so that people made bets on the number of drinks it would take for the license to appear, gambling that turned out to be truly random, since the license's appearance seemed—even to those who studied Two-Speed with the care that other men devote to a horse-racing program—to be dependent not on the alcohol in his system, but on the waverings of his heart and mind, waverings too complicated and chaotic for pattern or prediction.

Two-Speed would slap the license down on the scarred surface of the bar table and force his companions of the evening to stoop over it while one of his fingers, wrenched outward, pointed to the "A." Then, flipping the card over, he would read aloud the words on the back: "Classes: A: Tractor-trailer combination." After which he would challenge anyone within hearing to produce such a license, and when they all shrugged or ignored him, familiar with the routine, he would launch into a description of the testing, detailing its difficulties, and end by claiming that he had never failed to pass it, not even the first time.

Which, I have no doubts, was true. If there was one thing in which Two-Speed's integrity was absolutely sound, it was in his knowledge and handling of a truck—so much so that he often turned down jobs, claiming with complete forth-rightness that he wasn't sober enough. Two-Speed had no time for drunk drivers. He walked the mile from his house at the edge of town to the bar to ensure that when drunk, as he most surely would be later, he wouldn't be tempted to drive home. And he insulted those who staggered up from the table pulling their keys from their pockets, calling them damn fools and menaces to society, calling them bastards and killers and suicides, and went so far as to stand wobbling behind their vehicles, cursing them, daring them to back over him, the red glow from their brake lights enveloping Two-Speed's thin and crooked limbs and turning the smoke and steam from their exhausts, in the winter, into a cloud that seemed to burn internally, passing up over Two-Speed's form so that his curses, cracked and hoarse, emanated from the cloud.

His stubbornness was so great that he would, indeed, have let himself be run over, as evidenced once when Hank Tyrrell challenged him by slowly backing up until his bumper touched Two-Speed's knees. Two-Speed remained rooted, swaying as if in a strong, inconstant wind, without moving his feet. Hank backed further, and Two-Speed's knees crumpled. He fell to the pavement, into the red, glowing cloud, and remained there, damning Hank with all the obscenities at his muster. Still Hank backed up, in spite of the protestations of onlookers who, hearing the commotion, had left their drinks in the smoky bar to gather outside the door in the freezing air. Some of them waved their arms at Hank, trying to get his attention, but whether through the blinding obscurity of his stubbornness or of the frost on his windshield, he paid them no heed.

Two-Speed disappeared under the pickup until, depending on who you hear the story from, a scrap of his clothing caught on a rusted piece of metal or he grabbed onto the bumper and began to be dragged backward, his head hanging limply, scraping along. Never, though, did he shout for Hank to stop, but continued to scream like a crow that has learned to curse, his voice rising up from the exhaust, calling Hank to judgment for the menace he was to the roads, to the drivers who took their responsibilities seriously and knew driving as an honor and a privilege.

Hank backed the pickup clear into the street, reassured, though he couldn't see Two-Speed, by the health and vigor of his voice. He then put the vehicle into drive and began to leave the scene, puffed with pride, thinking Two-Speed had survived the backing-up and was out of danger and that he, Hank, had just become the first man in town to outdo Two-Speed's orneriness.

He made it a half block down the street to the stop sign at the highway before he became puzzled by two facts: first, that Two-Speed's voice was following him; second, that the herd of men milling outside the bar door was suddenly stampeding down the sidewalk parallel to his pickup, bellowing and pointing, most of them still in their shirt-sleeves, having never anticipated spending more than a few seconds in the frigid night. Hank could see them even through the layer of frost on his side window and decided not to pull onto the highway for home until he knew what had spooked them.

When he got out of his pickup to investigate, he found Two-Speed under the bumper, lying in blood that was beginning to pool from the great gash scraped in his scalp. Down the street, a steaming trail of the same blood marked Two-Speed's progress from the bar. Two-Speed did nothing to extricate himself from under the pickup, nor did he demand help or apology. Instead, looking up into Hank Tyrrell's horrified face bending over him, he accused Hank of being so drunk he would drag a man under his pickup, down the highway and into the night—"Proof!" he screamed, "that you're too damn drunk to drive and you got no right to be on the road in the condition you're in. There might be a woman on the way to the hospital to give birth to a baby, and you'd come charging down and kill them both. The last thing she'd see'd be your headlights in the wrong lane. How'd you like that, Hank? Would you like all that blood on the road?"

It was too much for Hank. He allowed his illusions of victory over Two-Speed to evaporate and, a defeated man, for the first time ever called his wife, admitted that he was too drunk to drive and had her come into town and retrieve him, sliding into the passenger seat beside her and refusing to acknowledge the friends who, delighted at his ignominy, waved to him from the door of the bar as his wife, stone-faced, pulled away from the curb.

When they finally managed to get Two-Speed out from under the pickup and standing, they discovered a great patch of skull, white but flowing with blood, showing through the matted hair at the back of his head. He declined offers of aid, shaking off the hands held out to him, pulled a dirty stocking cap out of his coat pocket, pushed it down over his head and walked, dignified but drunk, through the cold, wavering light of the street lamps, home.

The next day people came into town and looked at the trail of blood, frozen and brown against the black asphalt. They smoked and muttered and followed it, heads down, to where it broadened and spread near the stop sign, as if confirming, each one for himself, that yes, this had happened, reading their own individual interpretations out of the spoor. I was in town with my father, and, coming out of the hardware store, I saw the men huddled near the stop sign. I asked Dad what had happened, but he only glanced at the men and walked on to where he'd parked our pickup.

I had to run to catch him, and by the time I made it around the hood and had opened the door, he had the engine running. He was staring through the windshield at the brick-and-glass front of the Woolworth store. I sat down hard on the cold vinyl, hearing it snap under me and hoping it would crack and tear, shifting my weight more than necessary and looking at Dad. He glanced over at me, then jerked his head toward the stop sign. "Two-Speed Crandall about killed himself last night," he said. "But he didn't get the job done. They're"—he jerked his head again—"looking. That's all."

"That's *all*? Wow! How did—"

His eyes stopped me. "Just stupid."

He pulled the pickup onto the street. In spite of him, I leaned forward as we approached the stop sign, looking at the knot of men. They glanced up as we came near. A few nodded to my father. He nodded back, but we didn't join them, and I craned my neck backward as we turned onto the highway, watching them grow smaller through the rear window, and wondering what Two-Speed Crandall had done. I think I remember, though I can't be sure—and in truth, it seems unlikely I would—seeing the blood under the feet of the men, oozing out, a brown stain over which they floated, somehow supported by it.

I heard the story later through my friends and their older brothers, stories like that descending stratums until they finally reached clear down to groups of elementary students huddled on the playground. The stories also said that the next day Hank Tyrrell got a phone call from, of all people, LouAnn Crandall, but since Hank was outside feeding his cattle, LouAnn berated Hank's wife, Betty, demanding that she keep her husband away from Simon—Two-Speed's real name—and informing her that Simon was sick and in bed and that Betty had no right to let her husband nearly kill

LouAnn's husband. This phone call, by all accounts, did little to speed Betty's forgiveness of Hank, and he wasn't seen at the bar for several months after it.

These things are local legend. They've been filtered many times in being retold, and I remember them in the whole and connected way that we remember things from childhood, when even nursery rhymes have such reality and truth that we can ask our parents who the little boy who lived down the lane was, and where was the lane, and why did the black sheep want to give him some wool—questions that filled out and tried to make whole the disconnected phrases. If I tell these things with some fondness, it is fondness for the story, not for the man.

Or fondness, perhaps, for the enigma of the man. Or the enigma of memory. I remember Two-Speed still, sitting high in the cab of the semi when he came out to haul cattle for my father. To get to our barn, the drivers had to come into our yard, turn, and then back carefully between two grain bins, curve around a tree that my father refused to cut down, then straighten the rig out and ease up to the barn door. Most of the drivers would study the route, then, guided by someone else, would back up, get off course, go ahead, back up, gradually easing their way, by fits and starts, between the bins and around the tree. But Two-Speed would walk the route he had to take, then climb into the cab and back the trailer up, without ever going ahead or readjusting, or slowing down or riding the clutch. He would simply start, and there was something inexorable and beautiful about it, the churning engine, the diesel smoke, the crunch of gravel under the tires, the massive rectangular rig rolling backward, twisting without pause, reasserting its course, the exhausts throbbing, until the trailer, as wary and gentle as a dog meeting another, eased up to the chute and stopped with a sigh of air brakes, just touching the wood.

It mesmerized me. Done at night, as it often was so that the cattle would arrive at the stockyards in the morning, it was like waking from sleep to a bigger dream than any I could have dreamed myself, the whole semi glowing within the orange and red of its running lights, creaking and swaying over its axles. Then Two-Speed would take his eyes off the mirrors, where he had been intent and focused, and he would climb down from the cab, his pants tucked into his boots, as gaunt and stringy as a heron, with the same enigmatic glitter in his eyes, and the same careful delicacy about his walk, as if his world were one of shallow water and sucking mud, and walking in it was both risk and miracle. He'd step to the back of the trailer, and if he were more than an inch away from the chute, he'd grunt and spit and walk away, disgusted with himself.

But even before my father told me of Two-Speed's violence with his family, I was aware of a distortion that entered here. For Two-Speed would take out his disgust with himself on the cattle, wielding his prod with unnecessary vigor, shocking the steers even though they were moving well, shocking them just to see them jump, and holding the prongs against their flanks, holding them there when the cattle were jammed in the chute and couldn't move to escape the jolt. The steers would sometimes panic when he did this and fall to their knees on the slippery wood, their rear hooves booming in the barn as they struggled to rise, the blue arc from the blunt prongs of the prod sizzling in their hair, the sharp electric smell stinging my nostrils above the smell of oil and sweat and manure—and Two-Speed standing there unrelenting, a grim and dusky look on his face, the steer groaning in the closest sound to despair I've ever heard, until—it always happened, I waited for it, the tension building in me—my father, a man never given to swearing, or even to anger, would shout from across the barn: "Damnit, Two-Speed! Lay off the electricity!"

These are moments outside of time for me: the packed cattle like a live, roiling sea, and over their backs the two men staring at each other. Neither of them moved. The whole barn was moving, but the two men were stiller than posts or stone. My father's eyes, even in the diffuse yellow light of the barn, had that hard and distant cast that I'd noted as something borrowed from the horizon. I remember all this as something completely soundless, the cattle bucking and moving in silence, the chute swaying without creaking.

In Two-Speed's eyes there was the kind of look I had seen only once before, on the face of the neighbor's dog when, one night, I heard a commotion outside and, full of the exploratory courage of a young boy, took a .22 rifle and a flashlight and went to investigate. I found the dog tangled in a mass of barbed wire behind the chicken house, one of our chickens, feathers wet and bloodied, at its feet. Gashes along the dog's side materialized slowly in the tissue beam of the light I held. Its face, too, was cut, and blood flowed freely down its fur and into its mouth. I saw that even its tongue was cut; it must have been biting at the wire in its frenzy to free itself. It looked at me with the cunning and fear of a wild thing, but there was something else, too, that made me stop just as I was about to go to it and free its leg from the coil of wire. The eerie fear came suddenly upon me that this dog would kill me, or try to, should I free it. I don't know how long I stood there, the dark trees moving over me, before I put the rifle down and spoke the dog's name: Homer.

The animal relaxed, free to plead with me, to collapse into its daytime self, the pleaser of human beings. I see now that the flicker of hatred I had caught from its eyes sprang from an unbearable tension within it—its wild nature hating me for finding it helpless, its domestic nature hating me for finding it a killer. At the sound of its name, though, the dog became whole again, if not complete, and whined softly, giving in to the pain. I approached it carefully, and it waited patiently while I uncoiled the wire. Then it withdrew its legs, sniffed at the chicken lying in the barbs, looked once at me, and fled. With the light, I followed its limping form, receding between the dark trees of the grove, until it disappeared.

In Two-Speed's eyes as he stared at my father there was the same look the dog gave me, and it made me uneasy, an uneasiness I was then too young to recognize as fear for my father. But in the distant hardness of my father's eyes there was a look to oppose Two-Speed's—a steady, unwavering anger, so steady it was almost calm. I know now that his anger was concerned not only with the cattle, but also with the children, with those three boys not his own, and that he was enraged at his own helplessness, being as he was a believer in stories that were unproven and therefore impossible to act upon. Always it was Two-Speed who turned away. Always, with a show of sullenness he stuffed the prod into the pocket of his overalls, where it protruded stiff and ungainly, making him look even more like an unkempt wading bird as he stood undignified and lost in the dim, manurey air of the barn, where—in my memory—sudden sound resumes.

Two-Speed's funeral was a large forgetting. The whole town turned out for it. Men told all the old, good stories, slapping their hands down on the long church basement tables in imitation of the license that had flicked night after night from Two-Speed's pocket in the bar down the street. They laughed as they ate the hamburger-and-rice hotdish prepared by the St. Mark's ladies, and they slapped Hank Tyrrell on the shoulders as they walked behind his chair, while he, sitting next to Betty, pretended to ignore them. But everyone was grave around LouAnn and the three boys, men now like myself, who nodded their heads and accepted condolences without emotion, indifferent to all the attention being given them now that they no longer sought it. Everyone was careful, in speaking to the family, to call Two-Speed Simon, and to repeat the virtues they could be sure of—that no one drove a semi better than Simon Crandall, that the town would never see the likes of Simon Crandall's skill again.

I was there. I am, after all, one of them. I have been one of them since that day when my father brought me into adulthood by revealing the other stories. I was there, not to rejoice or mourn, but simply to remember, in the silences when the laughter died down, those stories no one told.

Easter Dresses

M Y children are so lovely. They are hiding, for now, in the upstairs room, but I hear them moving. I hear their feet, the birdchirp of their voices. It is like having birds in the house, sometimes like sparrows flittering, sometimes like pigeons. But heavier. The ceiling above my head creaks. Upstairs, the windows are open, the curtains blown inward by the wind. When my children are silent, I imagine they have flown away through those open windows. I even look outside, thinking I might see them there against the sky.

As a girl, I used to walk to an old cement bridge that crossed a drainage ditch. A culvert dripped water, gathered from the fields, into the ditch—dripped and dripped and dripped, even in the hottest weather. Minnows came and went, and frogs leaped from the tangled grass and splashed, speckles on their backs. But I went there to make the pigeons fly.

They roosted under the bridge. From far away, on the road, I heard their cooing. I thought of ghosts stirring in the summer sun. When I got closer, the cooing stopped. I'd stand on the bridge, on the hot gravel, and try not to breathe. I knew the pigeons were under me, their eyes open—bright, small, alert—the little breath of birds moving through the holes above their beaks. I'd reach down and take a stone, hold it over the water, then tip my hand and watch it fall. I tried to tell if the feather sound began before the stone splashed in the water.

Out they'd spread, like flowers growing in the sky, bursting from the bridge. They must have simply dropped from the girders—falling toward the water, then swooping upward as their wings caught air. Pigeons have such noisy wings, as if they beat them against each other, like small, feathered hands clapping, as they fly. All those wings under the bridge, and then the birds bursting out, rushing from their own wing sound, into the distant sky.

Henry's shooting of the dog has brought a pall upon the family. The children hardly eat. They stare at their plates and pass the food in silence. Lent is over, and I'm cooking good meals again; it hurts to see the children letting their food grow cold.

Henry knew that I was right, but he argued. That's why the children hide now, why they look at me as if I were a stranger. They avoid him, too, except for David, who works with him. He's grown so strong, David has. One day I saw him carry two bales of hay, one in each arm, from one barn to the other, clear across the farmstead. He never stopped to rest, and he's only fifteen. When he's grown, he'll be stronger than his father.

David and Henry are together always. But I see them walk across the yard toward the farrowing house, and it seems to me that David's head is too erect. He stares straight ahead. I don't see his head turn sideways, as it always used to, talking to his father. Children can make life so hard. The things you have to do—doubly hard and painful.

"The children love the dog, Maggie"—that's what Henry said to me. That was his argument—but he knew it wasn't sound. A dog that kills farm animals can't be allowed to live. It's almost a wild animal. If it were pigs that had been killed instead of chickens, Henry wouldn't have hesitated. He wouldn't have talked of love. I saw the children's eyes, the hope that lit in them when he said those words. He shouldn't have given them hope that way. It just made it harder on them when I had to remind him: *this has nothing to do with love; it is responsibility that matters here.* Terrible words, but I had to say them.

Once I tried to surprise the pigeons. I wanted to see how far they fell before they caught the air. I wanted to see their wings spreading, the flat fingers of their feathers wide and grasping, playing the limber air like a pianist plays a piano. I remember how the sun poured down on my back, how every step raised dust as I crept along the road. I lifted my foot like a ballerina, like a dancer on a stage, and touched my pointed toes against the gravel.

I walked like this into the ghosty cooing. It burbled out along the air. It seemed to change the light, to force a coolness into it—something like a shadow but not a shadow, a mist but not a mist. I reached the bridge and still the cooing came. I'd never managed that before. I was so silent, I didn't even breathe.

Then the grass confronted me, sloping down to the water. It was brown and full of dust, settled from cars passing on the road. Wild roses thorned their way among it. If I put even one foot into that grass, no matter how slow and pointed, the rustle would fall on those feathered ears. I knew that. I had no chance.

I ran into the grass, leaping down the ditch. My legs were magic—striding, downhill legs. The grass clutched at them and released its dust. I went so fast my pigtails flew around me. I looked sideways as I ran, watching for the pigeons, but they were fast beyond me. I saw one flash of wing dipping below the bridge, then cutting upward. One quick flash of white, converted light cast back into the shadows, gone in the instant of seeing it. Then, unable to stop, I splashed into the water and stood there panting, hearing the echo of wings.

I wore a blue dress to church yesterday—light blue, the color of sky. It was hard to find the money for it, what with four children now. Halfway through Lent, I thought I'd have to choose another. But egg prices went up two cents, and I skimped a little more on meals, and it was just enough.

It made me feel good to wear it, almost like my body didn't exist. It's funny how a good dress will do that. How you put it on and your body feels so clean and light you almost forget you have one. I came out onto the church steps. Everyone was wearing new spring clothes, and we were complimenting each other. A spring breeze rippled my dress hem, moving the cloth against my legs. I felt as if I became that breeze—as if I'd gone away into the sky at the same time that I stood there on the steps.

The first year I bought a dress from the egg money, Henry was surprised. He didn't understand. He never has. He's never known about my Easter dresses. For two years after the hailstorm, when I started to buy groceries with the egg money, I went without new clothes. I think I was numb. But the third year, I was in town, shopping, just as Lent began. I'd bought some jeans for Henry and was walking through the dresses on my way out of the store when I saw the first dress hanging from a rack. A fan above made it ripple. The cloth flowed like water. Something happened to me then, as I reached out to touch that waving cloth. (It was blue, though not all of them have been.)

When I tried it on, I found it hard to breathe, seeing myself standing in the circle of mirrors. I've never wanted anything so much. All I had was the grocery money from the eggs, but I laid the dress away with ten dollars of it and walked out of the store in a daze, thrilled to have done something so secret, something only for myself. At the grocery store I bought the cheapest foods, anything with bulk and small expense. No one asked questions, though; no one seemed to notice.

For two weeks I cut back on groceries, saving for the dress, before Henry said anything. Then, one time, when I placed food on the table, he just stared at it. I felt my face begin to heat. I went to the refrigerator for the milk.

"Maggie?" he asked. I didn't turn around. I looked into the white interior, almost empty.

"Yes?" I replied, trying to sound normal.

"What's going on?"

"What do you mean?" I'd forgotten why I went to the refrigerator. I felt the cool air against my face and leaned in closer.

"This is the third time this week we've had macaroni and cheese for supper," Henry said.

Then my answer came to me. My mind cleared. I picked the milk off a shelf and turned around.

"It's Lent," I said. "We're not supposed to be feasting." I said it quietly but hard, and held his eyes.

He almost replied. Then he looked down at his plate.

That was the end of questions. For the rest of Lent, we ate those meals.

Every week I put some more egg money away for the dress. David seemed to do fine. He didn't get weak or sick. And on Easter, when I wore the dress, Henry's eyes held me for a moment in the bedroom. I wanted him to say how much he liked it. I even hoped he'd ask me how I came to buy it. I wanted to tell him, to make him part, again, of how I looked. But he never asked. He let it be my business.

Still, his eyes changed. It was a bit like things were new again. A bit.

I wore the dress all day. I felt self-contained and distant, like my family and the rest of the world were below me. Like I was a world in myself, moving in my world. I knew this would go on. I knew there would be other Lents, other scarce, sacrificial meals, other dresses. The knowledge swelled in me like guilt, or passion, strong as the taste of salt, or the iron smell of blood.

Yesterday when we got home from church, the children scattered from the car. The two youngest looked for Easter eggs, the older ones guiding them. They were having such fun, so bright out there on the lawn: shouting, stooping, laughing with each other, finding the two-dozen eggs I'd dyed the night before, when they were in bed.

Then the laughing stopped. Completely. Henry had started for the house, to change clothes to check the sows before we had Easter dinner. He turned around and looked at me in that funny silence. Elsie ran from behind the house, her face dark and worried. "We found a dead chicken," she said. We followed her back around the house to where the children stood in a circle, looking down. David moved aside, watching me. At his feet lay one of my hens, its neck twisted back, its eye open, its feathers stained with blood.

"What the hell?" Henry said. Then: "Where's Critter?" He put it together faster than I could. I was still looking at the blood smeared on the feathers. As if I didn't know it was blood, didn't know the chicken was dead. A dead chicken made no sense on Easter morning after church, in the middle of an egg hunt, with the children laughing and me with a new dress on.

Suddenly Henry yelled, loud as he could: "Critter!" Coming in that silence, it made me jump. He yelled again, but the dog didn't appear. Henry strode off toward the chicken house. David glanced at me before following him. The rest of the children straggled after them across the gravel. I brought up the rear. I saw an egg the children had missed beneath a dogwood bush.

When I got to the chicken house, Henry was standing there, his arms hanging at his sides. The children grouped together, huddling around David. Scattered in the dust were mounds of feathers. Dead chickens. It might have been a quarter of the flock, these lumps of white, their feathers ruffling in the breeze. It was like a moonscape, white rocks plunked down in a desert. Dog-paw prints showed in the scuffled dust.

Henry called again for Critter. He moved among the chickens, stepping over them. I walked into the carnage, too, but the children stayed outside it. David had his arm around Marcia and was saying something to her. The dog didn't appear. A breeze came up, spewing dust over us, and the door to the chicken house blew open, banged, banged again. Inside, the living chickens clucked stupidly.

Then David called. His voice cracked when he called—it started out like Henry's but ended like mine. Right away there was a rustling in the grove, and Critter crept out, his tail between his legs. The little whites at the edges of his eyes showed as he glanced up at us. He slunk over to David. David hooked a finger around Critter's collar, and the other children formed a circle around the dog. When that circle closed, the dog relaxed. He lost all guilt. His tail made little motions in the dirt. His tongue came out, and he panted, pink and sloppy.

There was another time, several years ago. David was seven I know, because when this happened, he was wearing the little cowboy boots I'd bought him that he'd wanted so badly. Jacinta was six. We'd just gotten the new baby chickens from the hatchery, and the children loved them. We put peanut shells down in the brooder house and hung red heat lamps, and the chicks glowed red and yellow, like little flames. David found that knocking on the board we'd set up to hold the chicks in would bring them running, like to a mother's cluck. They'd crowd around his knock.

We had cardboard rounding out the corners. Without it, the chicks could cluster in fright in the corner and suffocate themselves. One day I went to water them—Henry was helping me, I don't know why—and we saw David standing outside the door, his face white. "Dave?" Henry said. "Is something wrong?" But David wouldn't respond. He just looked up at me, guilt on his face.

Then we got to the door and Henry uttered: "Christ!" and dropped his pail of water. It splashed both me and David, soaked into the ground. Henry ran into the brooder house. In the middle of the peanut shells Jacinta stood, holding a chick and cooing. She'd gone over the board to chase the chicks, and had knocked the cardboard down. A mass of chicks, frightened by her chasing, had crowded into the corner. They glowed there, quivering.

I came to the door, still holding my pail. Henry's big hands were thrusting down into the chicks like shovels or rakes moving through a liquid flame. Every time they came out of the flame, they scattered chunks of it before they plunged back in. I watched him. He worked so hard to save them—helpless things that wouldn't save themselves. Worked so hard to keep the balance he'd established. I didn't move. I wanted to let the chickens die, to kneel beside David and Jacinta and hug them, freed of that balance at last.

When Henry finally had the chicks cleared out, he stood in the corner to block it, and began to reinstall the cardboard. We all stood very still, until the chicks calmed down. There were dead ones lying in the peanut shells, but the living ones didn't notice. They walked right over them. I thought: *What kind of animal almost suffocates and forgets it in minutes?*

When he'd replaced the cardboard, Henry began to pick up the dead chicks. He took the empty water pail and dumped the dead ones in it. They filled half the pail. Unmoving, one on top of the other. Henry set it outside the door and finished feeding the rest.

I was outside with the children. Jacinta took my hand. "I'm sorry, Mommy," she said.

"Sweetie," I said, "you didn't know."

Then Henry came out. He looked at the horizon, took his cap off, replaced it. His eyes rested for a moment on Jacinta, then swept over me to David.

"Things sure do happen, don't they?" he said.

No one replied. The remaining chicks peeped and twittered. Jacinta held my hand.

"Well," Henry said, "we'll buy some more. It's a pretty small loss at this point."

Buy more. I let go Jacinta's hand. Henry never even looked at me.

"Things maybe happen," I said. "But I told David not to let Jacinta go across the board."

Before Henry could reply, I turned and walked away.

"You'll have to shoot the dog," I said. Henry stood in the middle of the carcasses. He looked up at me, but it was more like he was looking through me, like he didn't see me. The wind came cool and blew my dress around my legs, wrapped it in a swirl. The lace ruffled, lifting. It made no sense to be in my Sunday clothes—to be feeling like I might fly away with the wind—with dead chickens all around my feet.

Critter panted. David held his collar. The children waited.

"It's not the dog's fault, Maggie," Henry said. "He's not even a year old. Just a pup. He's never been trained."

I don't know why he argued. He's the one who always said you had to do what you had to do. Even if I wanted to relent, give up, he'd go ahead and do whatever it took. When that hailstorm hit and we had no insurance, he looked out the window at the devastation for days—and then began planting again, though it was too late. And in his head formed the means that would see us through, thought of these chickens, and egg money—as something new and separate, cut off from anything else.

And now he argued with me. All these chickens dead, all those eggs that would never be laid and never sold.

"Maybe it's not the dog's fault," I said. Henry felt the implication and looked over at the children. They refused to meet his eyes. David, though, looked directly at me, his gaze unflinching. "But the dog's fault or not, it'll happen again. It has the taste for blood now."

Before Henry could reply, David did. Again his voice cracked. "I must have left the door open," he said. "When I watered them this morning, I must have forgotten to latch it."

He didn't even blame the wind. Or the fact that he was in a hurry, what with Easter service and the need to get there early. He took full blame on himself. And he was lying, protecting Marcia. I saw her eyes go big at his words, saw her shuffle her feet. She's eight and is always leaving doors open. I stared at David, keeping my expression stern—but I felt so proud of him, protecting his sister that way, willing to shoulder a responsibility that wasn't even his. He never dropped his gaze, never wavered as he stared back at me.

"It happened," Henry said. "That's all. We'll just have to be more careful."

It was as if he refused to acknowledge what had happened. Refused to see the loss. Took on the role of protecting the children.

"We can't take that risk," I said. "The dog has to go. You know it as well as I do, Henry."

The children looked like statues. Only Marcia quivered a bit, like a captured bird. My heart went out to them. I hated myself.

For the first time since we'd come home, Henry fastened his eyes on me. As though he was seeing me, and the dress, and all of it. He saw me. Not merely the horizon, or the land. *Me.*

For a moment it was as though he'd forgotten where he was standing and what we were talking about. We looked at each other, and it seemed we were looking across our entire relationship, but his eyes saw me the way they did before the hailstorm and the chickens and the egg money—and I thought for a moment that things would be all right. Then the dog whined slightly, and Henry's eyes dissolved. They flickered to the children, rested there for a moment before going out to the whole flat land around us. And he said: "The children love the dog, Maggie."

My heart fell. Everything collapsed, and here he and I were, with our children, standing among dead chickens, and nothing had changed, and the only love he could talk about was the love the children had for the dog. I felt so sorry for us all, for how we'd gotten here.

"Love?" I said, bitter and despairing. "What does love have to do with this? It's responsibility that matters here."

The dog's panting became a bellows, slow and old, containing eternity, mixing breath into the world. Between those breaths Henry gazed off into the distance, and I watched him, waiting. Even the feathers of the chickens stopped moving.

Then Henry quit resisting me. He gave up. He couldn't take the step he needed to take, couldn't see it. My heart shriveled even more, though I didn't think it could, when his eyes met mine again, and I saw he was resigned—to necessity; to what he'd decided needed to be done.

Hail falls down from the sky. The opposite of birds—hard and cold, slick and smooth—it has no grip on the air. David was a baby when it happened. In the night, over the din on our roof, I heard him cry. I went to him, held him in the darkness while the hail pounded down. The whole house shook. I thought the hail might come through the roof and strip my baby from my arms. He fell asleep, but I couldn't put him down. I wrapped a blanket over him and held him, and fell asleep myself, in the chair, listening to his small, fast breath.

I awoke to silence. Still holding David, sleeping, I went to the window. The cornfield was a field of bones, stripped of all leaves. Like nothing would ever rise from that land again.

For two days Henry was silent. Even inside the house, his eyes were fixed on the land, as if the horizon had a claim on them. He sat always near a window. I tried to talk to him—I wanted to ask, and talk about, why we stayed on in a place where the sky poured down stone; I wasn't going to demand we leave, just talk about what had happened—but Henry didn't hear me. His eyes were taken by those bony fields.

Then two days after the storm, I was awakened by the sound of our tractor. I went to the window. Henry was hooking up the disc. For three days he disced, completing the destruction. There is no other way to hide the signs of hail. From the house, alone with David, I watched the tractor's exhaust smudge the sky. I grieved, but I understood what Henry was doing, why he would disc the fields up.

But then he did an insane thing. Without asking me. Once again I heard the tractor early, and through the window saw him hooking up the planter. My heart raced. A new crop would never beat the frost, not even soybeans. I dressed and went downstairs before I remembered to check on David, and ran back up. He was sleeping, though stirring slightly. The engine outside snorted, the tires crunched the gravel. I made up my mind. David stirred again, but I went down, put on my boots, and went out to the pickup. I choked it, and it wouldn't start. I hit the dashboard, bruised my hand, then closed my eyes and held the accelerator down.

By the time I got to the field, Henry had the planter in the ground. My small hesitation over David had given him time, and he was already raising dust. I stopped the pickup at the end of the field road and got out. I ran toward him, calling, but the engine hid my voice. I stumbled on the clods and fell to my knees as the tractor pulled farther away. I was crying and couldn't run. A wind came up and blew the dust, cleared the space between Henry and me. As he turned around, watching the planter, his eyes swept over me, and never stopped.

I fell again on the way back to the pickup. I wanted to just lie there in the dirt and sun until he returned on the round, but I knew I couldn't. Even before I opened the door to the kitchen, I heard the thin, high wail of our baby, reedy in the empty rooms.

We keep the gun in the broom closet. Henry had to take out the mop and broom before he found it. He slid it from the case, then reached up on the shelf for shells. The children wouldn't look at him, nor at me or each other. Only David seemed natural, leaning against the counter. When Henry turned around, the gun near his waist, David asked: "Should I go with you, Dad?"

He startled me. Nothing he'd said all morning was anything I expected. I prayed Henry would say no. David's the one who found the dog, picked him from the litter, took care of him.

"It's my job," Henry said.

He wouldn't look at me even to accuse me.

Marcia put her hands over her ears when she heard him call for Critter. Then she left the kitchen, and the other children followed her upstairs, trailing one another. Only David was left. We said nothing. He held a glass of water in his hand, let it dangle from his fingers. Finally, looking down at it, he said: "Mom, that dog. That dog could be . . . I mean, I could . . ." But he didn't finish. He set the glass down, then went upstairs to join the others. I heard them speak to him, and his voice replying, but I couldn't make out the words.

Henry spoke little to me all those days he was replanting, saying just once: "You do what you have to do, even if it makes no sense." I was horrified at his work, at how he never stopped, how his shirt, when he came in after dark, was stained with sweat, and even his leather belt was soaked. I didn't know a body could contain so much water. I marveled at him, too: that a man could think to fight the sky. But *why*?

Then he came to me one day while I was heating a bottle for David. He sat down at the table. "It's going to be hard," He said. "It's a tough time ahead of us."

I watched the bubbles form on the bottom of the pan. They hissed and rose. In the other room, David cried.

"We'll need to save every way we can," Henry said. "I'm just hoping this second crop makes it at all."

I had a terrible thought—that it might be good if it didn't make it and we had to start all over, somewhere else. I imagined us white and clean, blooming in a bright, blue land, with only echoes of our leaving remaining here. It was a terrible thought to think, after all the work he'd done.

But I could see it was terrible, so I kept it to myself. Why couldn't he see that what he said next was just as terrible? "I've got some ideas," he said. "We'll get chickens. That'll help. You'll take care of them. From the egg money, you can buy groceries. It'll be tight, but we'll get by. Anything left over from the egg money, you can use that for whatever. Good clothes for yourself. Dresses for yourself."

I turned around, not believing I'd understood him right. But he was staring out the window. Faintly in the glass I could see his reflection, but his eyes were lost.

"Henry?" I said.

He turned to me—but I saw I'd become part of the landscape. His eyes didn't take me in. They were still on the fields. Without even knowing it, he'd abandoned me to myself. What I was about to say faded on my tongue. Behind me I heard the bottle bang against the pan as the bubbles lifted and dropped it. I turned back to it without speaking, so as not to see Henry's eyes.

I tested the milk on my wrist. I couldn't feel it: the perfect temperature. David was screaming; I couldn't think straight. Maybe if David hadn't been so demanding right then, I could have thought of something. But I had to quiet him. I took the bottle in to him—and then I heard the screen door bang shut as Henry left the house, went back to his fields, and left me with the baby.

Left me, with my beauty—such as it is—in a balance with my baby's cry for food.

I watched as David guzzled the bottle, watched the milk flow and drain. I forced myself to hold it there, feeling who I was—or who I'd been—drain away with it, leaving me empty, a hollow, transparent shell, knowing Henry would never see that that's what I'd become.

I was staring out the window when I heard the shot. It made me jump, even though I was expecting it. Some pigeons that roosted in the silo flew up and spread against the sky. From inside the house, I couldn't hear their wings. The birds just floated out there, far away.

Upstairs, Marcia let out a little cry. I'll have to go to her in time, let her know the dog's death isn't her fault, comfort her, hold her, sing to her. There's so much sorrow here. How do you explain to a child that sometimes there's just too much sorrow, and it's not because of anything the child did?

Staring out the window, I saw the colored egg still lying under the dogwood bush. The entire Easter ruined. And it'd started out so happy. I can retrieve the egg later and make egg salad out of it, so that it doesn't go to waste. But if only one of the children could have found it.

The entire house went silent after Marcia's cry. I imagined the children flown away, like those pigeons, through those open windows. I wished for them that they could—fly away, from here, from all of this. In the sink, thawing, lay the carcasses of the chickens we'd taken from the freezer for Easter dinner.

Chickens are so ugly. Especially the old ones, the hens that lay the eggs. Their combs get gray, their rear ends go bald. They get lice, and their feathers get ragged and then fall out. They become completely ugly.

More than that, they can't fly. Their wings are short and weak, and their bodies are too heavy. When they try to fly, they look like some mistake. Their necks thrust out, their legs curl up. They get a few feet off the ground—that's all, though they beat the air ferociously. They look like cruelty in the air. When they try to land, they crash. They fall upon their breasts. God, I hate chickens. I wish the dog had killed them all.

The Husker Tender

THE Yellow Hats are servants here. They are the squeegee pushers and the shovel tenders, the standers on metal platforms. Closest to the chains and belts and blades, they are the ones who feed the machines, and the ones whose feet swell. Out in the fields, where the pickers move up and down the rows, sand flies navigate by heat and starlight, in silence, to find warm flesh, draw blood and raise lumps. Here there are no sand flies or stars. No silence. The Yellow Hats, if they talk at all, shout to each other, pulling out their earplugs and letting them hang on cords around their necks.

I move down the aisle, my blue hard hat firmly on my head. I watch the Yellow Hats, make sure they and their machines are working. If I'm walking toward the canning room, the huskers are on my left, the cutters on my right. At the beginning of each shift I feel the cement under my feet vibrating, but soon I no longer notice.

The women who work the cutters are college girls. This is summer work for them. They have dreams that take them far from this place—or else they wouldn't be here. They pull the corn from the bin in front of them, turn it so the tapered end of the ear faces the spinning, circular blades of the cutter, push it so the machine catches it, reach for another ear. They do this endlessly, all night. The shorn, sweet kernels fall onto one belt, the bare cobs onto another, one going to the canning room, the other to a refuse pile where trucks appear in the night to haul cobs and husks away.

Everyone gets a five-minute break every hour, ten minutes every other hour. That's state law, five and ten. Sometimes I sit on the metal steps leading upstairs to where college boys push corn off the upper belt and down into the huskers, with their whirling rubber rollers. I sit on the steps and smoke and watch the college girls and keep my eye out for White Hats, who sometimes appear unexpectedly, pretending to be going from one place to another, but who are actually on missions of distrust, spying. If I see a White Hat, I stand up in the shadows and pretend to be just coming down the steps from an inspection. I drop my cigarette onto the refuse belt below me.

This is summer work, lasting only as long as the corn in hundreds of contracted fields lies between the milk stage—when it's too soft and the cutters would turn it to mush—and the point of being overripe and hard. The work pays well, but no one wants to do it, and no one really needs it. That's why there's so little trouble. There are small acts of rebellion; two or three times a summer the whole plant will shut down because a rock has gotten into the machinery. The White Hats curse then, and I curse with them for a while, because I'm a Blue Hat and align myself according to the situation, and because I'm the one who has to crawl into the machinery with wrenches and hammers to fix and straighten. But once down there, working with a trouble light in semi-darkness, I smile. The whole plant is quiet. I can hear the sounds of murmured voices, everyone quietly talking. The White Hats pretend the stone was carelessness and blame the people who work The Belt, picking out the corn smut and insects and stones and diseased ears. The White Hats will maybe even threaten to fire someone on The Belt unless more care is taken, but they, like everyone else, know it's a useless threat, just keeping up appearances, and that the rock was deliberate, not an accident, a way to relieve monotony, and they'll never catch who did it.

Everyone also knows that the whine of belts and the clatter of chains will begin again, the thud of corn falling down chutes. The only price anyone will pay for the hours of silence is the price everyone pays—the corn keeps coming in, piles up in the yard, and has to be dealt with. This is a place that people endure. And they can endure it because they don't need it. And because they're young, with their dreams all in the future.

The personnel office seldom makes mistakes. It hires jerk-offs and slack-offs all the time, and people who drink on the job and spit in the cans and take naps on pallets in the ware-house, and do as little as they can. But only once that I know of did it hire someone whose dreams were all behind him.

He showed up one night, working the automatic huskers. There are twenty, and each husker-tender is assigned five. He has a long-handled squeegee and a shovel. The corn, from above, comes thumping down into a bin, is straightened out by chains and grooves, and drops onto the rubber husking rollers. The husk is ripped off, and the newly naked ear bumps down the rollers and onto the belt that carries it down the line of huskers, up and over the aisle, and to one of the sixty college girls working the cutters.

The husks shoot off the rollers and pile up. With his squeegee and his shovel, the husker-tender goes from one husker to the other of the five under his care and pushes the husks into a hole onto the refuse belt below. Most husker-tenders let the husks pile up until they nearly reach the bottom of the machine, and then, with a little exertion, all at once push these large piles down the hole. The rest of the time they lean on the rail and watch for crosswise ears stuck in the rollers, or turn around and stare at the backs of the college girls, and think the thoughts that keep them awake.

The White Hats generally assign the new people to jobs and let us Blue Hats discover it. This guy appeared one night, working the five huskers at the end of the line, underneath the steps. And was he working them! I'd never seen anything like it in the plant. He made me laugh. He was short, maybe forty, with a bushy mustache and a potbelly and a small head, so that the adjustments on his yellow hard hat had to be pulled tight, and the hat seemed to float above his face like a plastic flying saucer.

But anyone can look odd here. What made me laugh was the effort this guy exerted to keep the floor clean. He looked like a small, efficient robot, a machine himself, going from one husker to the other with his squeegee and with quick, jerky movements, pushing tiny piles of green husks down the hole. He swept the cement as if it were a kitchen floor. Then as soon as he turned to the next husker, the floor he'd just finished was littered again. From the other end of the building, down by the manual huskers, I saw him going fastidiously back and forth, serious and intent on a hopeless job.

I laughed, but it was kind of pitiful. Only someone who thought he could lose his lousy job, and was desperate to keep it, would make it even lousier by working that hard. And when he saw me moving toward him, he worked even harder, glancing down the aisle with a nervous, rabbity twitch, then pretending he hadn't seen me and attacking the piles with renewed ferocity to impress me with his vigor and devotion, his hard hat slipping and wobbling on his head. Though it made me laugh even more, it also pissed me off—as if I were an enforcer or a White Hat, as if I were doing anything more than getting through the summer myself.

Still, I should have let him be. If he wanted to spend his nights attacking every single wasted husk as if it were a threat, why should I care? I guess it seemed too pitiful to me that someone his age should be so desperate. All the other husker-tenders regarded their machines with disdain. Though they served them, their attitude, at least, was superior to them. Maybe I wanted that from this guy, too. For a day or two, sitting on the steps in the shadows, I watched him. Everything that was mindless about the place, everything that was timed and cogged and driven, seemed summed up in the dip of his shoulders as he hunkered his weight against the squeegee, bobbing his head, jerking his knees. As I watched, my own muscles tensed trying to slow him down, trying to make him resist the grinding relentlessness of the place. I'd shake my head and start to watch the girls again, but even their sweet asses weren't enough to distract me. His movements always drew my eyes, ruining my solitude on the steps, and I'd feel the metal vibrating through my spine, and hear the roar even through the earplugs.

Finally one night I walked down the line of huskers on my usual rounds, seeing this guy glance over his shoulder as I came, his frenzied pace becoming more frantic with each step I took, the whole plant seeming to increase in frenzy with him, until I had the feeling that if I began to run, he'd go berserk and the entire plant would shake itself apart with him and collapse in a rush of broken glass and crumbled brick and twisted, green-painted metal.

When I stopped and leaned over the railing, he pretended to be too absorbed in the limp, green piles of husks to notice. I stood, waiting for him to glance over his shoulder to see if I'd gone, and when he did, I motioned to him with my fingers. A rodentlike gleam of anxiety brightened his eyes. He gave two more pushes with the squeegee, glanced at me again, saw I hadn't moved, gave one more push, like a machine running down, and finally turned and came as close to the railing as he could, the canvas belt, heavy with husked ears, moving slowly between us.

I reached my hand across the belt and shouted: "I'm Darrin Beckman."

A husk caught on a roller, flapped around once, went sailing over my head. His eyes darted into mine, darted away. He reached out a small hand, hairy on the back. He had no grip. It was like pressing foam insulation. He said something, I suppose his name. I jerked out my earplugs. The factory howled and screamed around me. "Sorry!" I yelled. "I didn't catch that."

I didn't catch it the second time either, only a slur of speech lost in the great sound around us, perhaps a Southern accent in it. I nodded, pretending to understand. "Glad to meet you," I yelled as loud as I could.

He didn't reply, glanced nervously at the machines behind him, spewing their waste. He seemed to think I was trying to trap him.

"You're working too damn hard," I shouted, smiling.

His face went blank, suspicious. I kept smiling and leaned farther over the railing that separated us. "Shit, this isn't a hospital," I yelled. "You don't have to keep it spotless. Just get the husks down the hole once in a while." I waved my hand down the row of huskers, indicating the other tenders, half of them gazing placidly at the girls.

He just stared at me. Behind him, the piles of husks grew. They snapped sodden off the black rollers, spraying juices. The yellow ears bobbed down the slight incline of the rollers, one after another after another, dropped off the edge, moved away down the belt. Another husk flew off, barely missing us. The guy's eyes didn't leave my face, and his expression registered no understanding. I felt my smile fading. Finally I shrugged, feeling kind of stupid, and angry that he'd made me feel that way. "Well, whatever," I yelled. "You do what you want."

As if released from a terrible obligation, he turned and attacked the first pile of husks with his squeegee. His back muscles strained under the wet, white T-shirt. I shook my head and walked out the side door. *Goddamn stupid yo-yo,* I thought.

The night was close and muggy, the stars lost behind the mercury and sodium lights of the yard. Inside the bare fluorescence of the cafeteria with its chipped cement walls, a few people sat at long, folding, steel tables, in small groups, drinking coffee or Coke, saying little, staring. I ordered a coffee-to-go, went back outside and leaned against the wall of the plant, feeling its vibrations, its endless mutter, coming to my ears through my spine.

The eyes I'd seen staring back at me, coal-black and blank, wavering as if on some off-balance internal gyroscope, had betrayed no spark of understanding, no human curiosity, no regard. I shrugged. The guy was probably a moron. It wouldn't be the first time the personnel office had hired one. I smoked and thought of the fields, the picker crews out there in the dark, under pure stars not lost in muddy light. I remembered how, before they'd promoted me to factory Blue Hat, I'd wait with a full hopper for the trucks to come, the tractor engine off, and coffee tasting so damn good in the cool night breeze. I looked down at the coffee in my cup, turned to brown sludge by the sodium light above me, then flung it. It sprayed, gleaming amber, and stained the gravel.

Dammit, Beckman, I thought to myself, *that was lousy work, too, and you know it.* I remembered the sand flies, the vicious welts they'd raise, loving the warm skin of the neck and scalp. I never knew they were there until they bit, and then it was too late. Their welts lasted for days, sometimes weeks, great soft lumps that sometimes oozed clear fluid. Hell—being a Blue Hat at the factory paid more, and I stayed dry when it rained.

I imagined the guy inside the plant, probably still scurrying around. *What a yo-yo,* I thought. *Yo-yo.* I laughed. A good name, since I'd missed his real one.

When I went back inside, nothing had changed. The college girls still stood in a long, diminishing line of shoulders and butts, shifting from one foot to the other, their hands moving methodically from bin to cutter to bin, unaware of the husker-tenders watching them. The corn went on dropping, thumping, snapping, spraying. And Yo-yo went on jerking, dipping, bobbing, more in tune with the machinery than ever.

Then, over the course of the next week, he began to slow down. I would sometimes see him stop work and look around, then feverishly attack the refuse under his machines again. Gradually these pauses got longer. He'd hold his squeegee with both hands, his round, blank face looking down the row of huskers, as if he were for the first time seeing where he was. Always, though, he stood among the machines, like a hostler among his horses.

Then one day I got up from fixing a broken chain on a manual husker and was wiping my hands on a terry cloth, and I glanced down the row, and there he was, leaning on the railing. He'd finally crossed the walk that led from his five machines to the aisle. In the bright lights over the aisle he looked even smaller, rounder, and his yellow hat seemed larger—large enough to drop and engulf him.

So my words had had an effect, I thought. A little slow on the uptake, but still. It was a relief not to have to see the mindlessness of the plant concentrated in his frenzy.

But within a week he began to cause trouble. He had no balance. He either worked too hard or he didn't work at all. And he either didn't understand or didn't care about the one all-pervading but unspoken rule of the plant: you could do almost anything as long as you didn't screw up another person's break.

Once he'd crossed the aisle and relaxed in his work and realized he didn't need to impress anyone to keep his job, he began to take breaks twice as long as he was allotted. The relief man couldn't get to the other tenders on time. I felt unrest growing among them. And Yo-yo, when he was working, now watched his huskers with a stubborn sullenness and anger, leaning against the railing but never relaxed. The other tenders crossed the walk between aisle and machines unconsciously, as part of the routine, the same boredom pervading their postures in either place, but Yo-yo crossed like someone forced, and he grabbed the handle of his squeegee as if to strangle it.

It half-amused, half-worried me. I'd been watching people do their jobs long enough to sense when trouble might take shape. Finally it came to the surface. I was back by the tool cabinet, out of sight of the huskers, when Nate, the relief man, slipped around the corner. I knew right away he'd waited for me to come back here, and I knew what he was going to say.

"I don't want to get anyone in trouble. But that older guy on the end huskers, he's taking twenty-minute breaks. It's really starting to piss people off."

When Yo-yo took his next break, I followed him to the cafeteria. He was standing at the counter when I came through the door, and I went up and stood beside him. When the girl brought him his coffee and doughnut, I signaled her: "I'll pay for that. And give me the same."

He glanced up into my face. I didn't smile this time. "Thanks," he mumbled through his mustache. Still, the thanks appeared genuine, and I felt a moment of regret. He seemed to have no friends at the plant, and I wasn't buying his coffee to make him one of mine.

We didn't say anything until we'd sat down and removed

our hats and placed them on the table. We sipped coffee for a while. Finally I said: "You took me too seriously."

I couldn't read his look. "Whad ya talkin' about?" I had to strain to catch the words even in the silence of the cafeteria.

"Well, shit," I said. "There isn't a whole helluva lot to do with those huskers, but what there is, you gotta do. There's no sense working your ass off. But you gotta do your job."

He stared at me. I had the strange feeling he thought I was betraying him. It made me angry. He was the one screwing up. "Shit," I said, "the relief man can't do your work for you. He's got other guys to get to."

Something sparked. He took a quick slurp of coffee. His face twitched. "The relief man's 'n asshole!" His eyes met mine quickly, moved away.

I had to conceal surprise. My face impassive, I thought: *So things have gone this far already. Nate must've said something before coming to me. Already I'm too goddamn late. I should've stepped in earlier, when I suspected trouble coming.*

"Nate's no asshole," I said calmly. "He has to make his rounds. If he's kept too long at one station, someone down the line misses a break. That's all. There has to be a schedule."

I was talking like a White Hat, and I knew it. But I could have been talking to the wall. He didn't seem to hear a word I said.

"Smart-ass college kids, think they know't all. Fuckers don' deserve breaks. You tell 'em bastards t' leave me alone 'f they don' wan' trouble."

What'd been going on here that I hadn't seen or heard? I thought that from my perch on top of the steps, or from walking the aisle, I saw pretty much everything, not only the larger picture, but the individual comings and goings—who took breaks together, who was friends with whom, even who was romantically involved, and certainly where the spots of tension were, the trouble and the nerves. Yet something had been building here, had already broken, and was hurrying me down a channel I not only hadn't chosen, but didn't even know existed.

For a moment I clearly saw Yo-yo's disgust for his work and for the college boys, who really were smart-asses, many of them, and who didn't need the money and were free in a way that he might not be. He thought the same disgust dwelt in me, since I was a little older. Maybe he thought I was stuck in this job, like he was, with no place else to go. It had never occurred to me that he might be seeing me the same way I saw him. In spite of the threat carried in his words, there was something confidential in his tone, as if he saw in me an ally.

I felt for a moment like chewing him out, showing him the difference in our positions. But it wouldn't solve the problem. I kept my face blank and thought for a second. "All right," I said, "they're smart-asses. Fine. All I'm saying is, you got trouble, keep it out of the plant. Just do your job. It keeps us all from getting our asses in a sling. And I'll talk to Nate, too."

Nothing. A stare like an animal about to bite.

"All right?"

He nodded his head and mumbled something that might have been yes.

I stood up. Suddenly he twisted in his chair and lifted the arm of his T-shirt, revealing a tattoo high up on the biceps. "Know what that is?" he asked.

The scattered groups of Yellow Hats at the tables were

watching us, glancing over, murmuring among themselves. I drew back. There was something about this little guy's manner and tone, boasting, but partly—there's no other word for it—intimate. He was showing me something he showed to few people. It's not what I'd come to him for. I didn't want to know his secrets. I didn't want to know what gave him pride or caused him pain. Standing behind my chair, my hands on its back, I glanced at the tattoo and shrugged. The fluorescent light struck off his sweaty arm, but I made no effort to get a better look. I never really saw it.

"That's a Hell's Angels tattoo," he said, raising his elbow so he could look at the insignia. His glance and voice seemed almost shy, even awestruck. Then he looked up again, and the boast came back to his words. "You tell that relief man an' the resta them smart-asses who they're dealin' with."

I might have responded out of simple curiosity if he hadn't spoken this last sentence, might have looked at the tattoo, even asked a question or two. But his brag, his tough-guy pose, pissed me off. "I'll tell them," I said, unimpressed, and walked away.

I talked to Nate and watched them both more carefully. Yo-yo took his breaks like he was supposed to, and Nate kept on schedule. I thought I'd repaired the damage.

Which only showed how little I understood him, how little any of us did. We, who did our jobs for the simple reason that they were jobs, could understand neither his previous dedication nor his present hatred—and now I think they were the same thing. I watched him watch the corn roll off the huskers—watch not impassively like the other tenders, who had grown up around here and knew that once the harvest of anything started, it just went on until it was finished—but with his round face moving and twitching under his hard hat, a scowl twisting his features every time a wild husk flew into the air, and I began to develop the feeling that he resented not so much the work itself, but whatever was inevitable about it—the faraway, unseen pickers moving up and down the rows, the trucks creaking on dark roads, the husker chains forever coming around, working the ears out of the bins, the rollers stripping the ears in a bright moment from green to yellow, the corn forever falling, until it seemed the machinery ran because the corn came through it, and the corn came through because the machinery ran.

I think that around two or three in the morning everyone felt that way in the plant, to some extent. But Yo-yo seemed to have no resistance to the feeling. He couldn't shrug it off and wait for the night, and then the summer, to end. The noise of the plant seemed to have worked its way into his heart, and it clamored in there, enraging him.

For a while, things were better, and then it all started over again. Yo-yo extended his breaks, slightly at first, not enough for me to say anything. Then he extended them more. And then, before I could do anything about it, Nate must have said something, for I heard a rumor: Yo-yo had called Nate out, would be waiting for him after work, to fight fair or dirty, with fists or knives or motorcycle chains, any way Nate wanted it.

It had the potential to be a joke, something to laugh about over beers. There are strange little tough guys in every small town, and Cloten is no exception, adolescents who never grew up, like bantam chickens always picking fights. But they're known elements. Sometimes they win a fight, sometimes lose; their noses are bloodied, they lie on the street or on the middle of the softball field after a game, fighting after the lights are turned off and the cop has gone someplace else. But people learn to ignore them, to walk away from them, even, in a strange way, to protect them, not letting them get hurt too badly and not letting them hurt anyone else too badly. The town even takes a certain character from them, denying and claiming them both.

But Yo-yo was an unknown, and this meant we couldn't laugh. No one knew who he was or where he came from or why he'd shown up here. No one even knew his real name. Lon was big and strong enough, had been throwing hay bales around since he was ten, but these are nothing in the face of true viciousness. And perhaps Yo-yo was truly vicious. We didn't know, and had no way of knowing.

So once more I went to him, for reasons I could only guess at: maybe to prevent injury, or to save him from embarrassment. I didn't know. In the cafeteria I sat down, this time without coffee, and we stared at each other.

"What the fuck you think you're doing?" I asked.

He didn't answer. Perhaps he feared me just a bit.

"This isn't a goddamn gang war," I said. "Nate's a good worker. I don't care what you think of him. Picking fights around here's a good way to get fired."

It was a small hope—that I could give him a reason to back down. He'd need a reason.

It didn't work. "No one fuckin' fires me!" It was an explosion.

A pause, a breath.

"I need this goddamn job! I got a wife, 'n I need this job, so don' you fire me."

A wife? *Him?* How did a woman fit into this? I was taken

aback, but I didn't have time to make sense of it. I had to deal with the man right now. I let myself be angry. "I'll fire you if I have to," I hissed. "And you keep this shit up, I'm gonna have to."

We were close to each other, leaning across the table, our voices low. People watched us. Yo-yo leaned closer. I smelled the coffee on his breath, smelled his sweat, and the scent of raw corn.

"I got friends," he said. "All these assholes think they're too good t' talk t' me. But I got friends."

It was almost pathetic. He had to convince me he had friends?

But he went on, his voice mean and surly. "You fire me, 'n I make one phone call. In a week there'll be a hunnert, two hunnert, Harleys in this town, with mean bastards ridin' 'em. We'll rip this place apart. So don' you fire me. I need this goddamn fuckin' job."

It was supposed to be all threat, but I heard the plea, the strange, surprising concern that he'd revealed only a moment before—the woman, the wife. But even the threat seemed extravagant. I was sick of this odd little guy, and sick of the way he eluded me.

"Bring your ugly friends," I replied. "You know what they'll find? The streets of this town lined with men holding baseball bats and crowbars. Everybody in this town's damn near related. Jesus Christ, you think they're going to sit around and watch you rip it apart? Bring 'em on, and see what happens."

My own story was as outlandish as his. Or maybe both of them could turn out to happen. I didn't know, and Yo-yo didn't know either. In our ignorance, we were equal. We looked at each other, breathing hard. Then I leaned away from him and let the tension break. I took a deep breath. "Look," I said, "no one wants to fight. You'd probably beat the shit out of Nate. I'm asking you not to. For his sake, even if he is a smart-ass. And for myself. Okay?"

I nearly added, "And for you," but thought better of it and reached my hand across the table.

I held it there for a long time while he looked at me, his gaze for the first time steady. Without his hard hat on, his bullet head seemed even smaller, with his hair, wet with sweat, matted against his scalp. I waited while he gazed at me, feeling desperate, somehow controlled by him, though I was supposed to be in control. I hid my despair, kept my hand extended, inviting him to take it.

Finally he did. He said nothing, but his grip was firm, and he held it for several seconds. Then he released me.

We fired him anyway. I didn't—it was a White Hat—but I have to say "we." It was probably inevitable. Maybe if I'd never said a word to him, let him scurry from husker to husker like he did when he first started, he'd have been fine, but I think something else would have happened. I don't know the specific reason he was fired. The White Hats must have heard he was causing trouble. I should have been the one to pass along such information, but rumors run in various channels and you can't keep track of them all.

On the night before he was fired, while I was sitting in the shadows on the steps, I saw a woman, small and pretty, her blond hair tucked up into her hard hat, come and stand beside him and watch his huskers with him. They both leaned on the rail. I sat very still. She never spoke a word but merely stood with him. She must've been on her break. After ten minutes, the two of them just standing there, she reached out and touched him. It seemed the most loving gesture I'd ever witnessed, just the tips of her fingers on his shoulders. She said something then that I couldn't hear, only a few words, and he looked at her and nodded. They both were very calm. I suspect that whatever caused him to be fired had already happened.

Then she straightened and looked right at the place where I was. I don't know if she saw me. But she seemed to look right into my eyes. I felt like a fool, transfixed and pinned—though, dark as the steps were, all she probably saw was shadow. Then she let her hand slide off his shoulder and turned and walked away.

I don't know why she loved him. He was as unlovable a man as I've ever met, and even if I didn't really know him, what I did know had to be a large part of who he was. Yet for ten minutes I saw him calm, even sweet, not wound up and not wound down, but at rest somehow—in her.

The next night we fired him. He worked out the shift and was gone, and she, too, I heard. The corn kept coming in, and I continued on my rounds. Things ran on schedule. A week passed, then two, and no Harleys boomed up the highway from Clear River, their lights a string of beads on the road. For a while, cafeteria talk was uncertain, or even tense, on this topic, but when nothing happened, the story turned into something else to remember and laugh about, along with Yo-yo's mustache and the hard hat that overwhelmed his face.

But I found it harder and harder, as the summer pro-

gressed, to sit and smoke in the shadows. There was something wrong in the bored, placid look of the boy who
replaced Yo-yo, in his willingness to do enough, but only
enough, to survive the summer, as if he'd discovered instinc-
tively the efficiency of the machines he watched, and slipped
into their cogwork demands without discomfort. I couldn't
stand to watch him. Every night when I arrived, I hoped for
a rock to make it through The Belt.

I'd find myself thinking about Yo-yo and his wife. No
one had seen them leave, but they must have gone on a Har-
ley. That much of his story had to be true. With the plant
booming around me, I'd think of them in the dark, both
helmetless, she straddled behind him, under the stars, her arms
around his waist, both of them going nowhere but into the
narrow beam of their headlight.

Light in the Crossing

M Y father died under a hawk. We had been getting the spring-tooth harrow ready for fieldwork when he handed me the welding wand, saying only "Bobbie"—without even finishing the request. He had always called me Robert, not Bobbie, but I didn't notice that at the time—all I saw was his acknowledgment that I could do a better job than he could. I took the wand that he passed, put his helmet on and turned up the amps on the welder, which he always ran too low.

I began to run long, smooth beads up and down the shares, enjoying the way the metal flowed and solidified like a fossil. Then, changing rods, I glanced out the shop door and saw him standing in the middle of the yard looking up, his hands at his sides. He was always checking out the sky, for weather or birds, but if he stopped moving to do it, he usually placed a fist on a hip. When I saw his hands limp at his sides and his face to the sky, I felt something serious and dark. I snapped off the welder and stepped out of the shop.

A hawk was circling overhead, so at first I was satisfied. My father liked hawks. Everyone else in those days called them chicken killers and shot them if they could, but Dad—trusting himself more than he did the stories—always said he'd never seen a hawk kill a chicken. He would be willing to stake a chicken out, he said, just to see if it'd make a hawk stoop. This one was a buteo, a red-tail—I saw red light flicker as it inclined and turned against the sun. When I looked back down, my father still stood there.

The official time of Dad's death was three days later, in a hospital, after he'd had another, more massive stroke. I don't count those three days. The last word he said was "Bobbie," and the last thing he saw—and by this I mean *recognized*—was the red-tailed hawk above him, circling.

After Dad died, for the first time since I had been old enough to carry a bucket, I had time on my hands. My mother rented the land to a neighbor. I told her I could farm it, but she was adamant in her refusal. Dad had never stopped working. "You're going to college," she said. "I'm not going to have you ruin that." I still had the cattle to feed—they wouldn't be sold until fall—but once I'd done the morning and evening chores (and, on Saturdays, ground the corn), I had time to myself.

On Saturday nights, I took my mother's car and went to Cloten. When Dad was alive, I had always asked, but the first time after the funeral, I just announced it. When I took the keys off the hook near the door, Mom said nothing. She merely looked up from her chair and watched me. I shut the door, feeling an inexplicable anger.

Then I began to go into town whenever I felt bored—at first just on Saturdays, then Fridays, then during the week. On Saturdays there were other teenagers there, driving up and down the streets looking for each other, but during the week, the town lay lifeless. I'd cruise the empty streets, then drive back home, hoping that Mom had finished her Rosary and gone to bed. I couldn't stand the way she looked at me.

One night I dreamed that I was walking a tightrope over a river so far below me that it was no more than an inky ribbon. The tightrope shivered. A high, cold wind blew. Then Mom appeared, standing where the tightrope was anchored. She had that look on her face, the look that always made me feel she wanted to—but could not—speak. But in the dream she spoke: "Good-bye, Bobbie." Then I slipped, and she watched me fall until I woke.

On one of those empty Wednesday nights, as I drove around, I passed a car I didn't know. When I looped back on Main, I passed it again and recognized Tony Schwartz. I knew little about Tony or his family except what I'd heard from others. His parents were divorced (at a time when people didn't get divorced in the farm country of Minnesota), and he lived with his mother. We sort of knew each other, of course, but only in the way that everyone in a small school knows everyone else. Tony was a poor student; I was a good one. I did know that he was often either nervous and fidgety or else so quiet at his desk that he inspired awe. Sometimes after class, when most of us were milling around, Tony would sit with wide-open eyes staring at the front of the room as if still absorbed in a lecture. Eventually someone—usually

Meryl Hills or Nate Untermeyer—would walk by him, whack him on the back of the head and yell: "It's morning, creep." But even Meryl and Nate always approached him from behind, away from those wide-open, still eyes.

At least once a week, however, Tony seemed to seek out trouble. He would call Meryl or Nate names quietly as they walked by, or try to trip them—always without show, as if he were absorbed in something else. Then he suffered their blows, maintaining a nervous grin as they bent his arm behind him or bruised his biceps with their fists. Once they stuffed him in his locker and shut the door. Tony never yelled, never even knocked. A whole class period went by before someone told a teacher. By the time the janitor let him out, Meryl and Nate were terrified, and the whole school was afraid he had suffocated. Tony stepped out of the locker, eyes wide, and smiled without seeming to see any of us. He refused to tell the principal who had done it.

I had never seen Tony in town before that Wednesday, but the next time our cars passed that night, I waved and he waved back. And when our paths crossed again, we pulled into parking spaces and stopped. He came over and slid through my passenger door. For a minute or so we sat there, staring at the dark plate-glass front of Angel Finn's hardware store. Finally I said: "Howdy, Tony."

"Robert," he said. That was the first time either of us had ever spoken the other's name.

"Got any ideas?" I asked.

"Just driving."

"How about down to the river?"

"Sounds good."

I drove north, the windows open on both sides, our elbows out, both of us silent. Then I turned onto the gravel road to the Minnesota River. Stones spat and skittered under the tires. Around curves the headlights shone into the woods and pastures, plucking the eyes of deer from the dark. Bugs rained from the edge of night, then thudded, smearing the windshield. We were engulfed by the bottomland smell of rot, the clean smell of distant skunk, the rising and falling sound of frogs.

I drove for an hour, as far as Fort Ridgely Park, where the Dakota Indians had rebelled in 1862. On Sundays, between cultivating corn and harvesting oats, Dad had often brought us here on picnics. After eating, Mom would rest and read, but Dad and I would wander through the museum, looking at Indian arrowheads and old rifles and swords. I always stared for a long time at the picture of the thirty-eight Indians they had hanged in Mankato after the uprising. They were arranged on a square gallows, nine or ten on each side, and around the gallows stood square ranks of military men, and behind them, the watching citizens. I tried to imagine how those Indians felt with white bags over their heads, the ropes touching their necks.

The previous summer Dad and I had looked at that picture together. "That was a bad deal, Robert," he said. "They just wanted to keep their land and families." I'd nodded, not knowing what to say, but I'd remained curious as to what the Indians had been feeling and whether being *made* to die was different than just dying.

I turned onto the park road, but the metal bar to the entrance was down. We read the park regulations in the headlights. Mosquitoes drifted into the car. "Ever been here?" I asked Tony.

"Lots."

"Seen the museum?"

"Who hasn't?" He looked at me with those strange, large eyes.

I wanted to see that picture again. Night and loss had settled into me and I had the feeling that maybe now I'd understand those hooded heads and the waiting crowd, that they'd speak to me this time. I thought of asking Tony if he'd sneak into the park with me, even though the museum was obviously closed. Then his eyes told me he was lying, that he'd never been here.

I honored the lie. "Yeah," I said. "I guess." I backed away, swung the headlights over the trees, turned onto the gravel. He must have known I'd detected the lie. He turned fidgety, seemed to want to speak. Once, when a large moth jittered into the lights, streaked erratically, and smashed into the windshield, Tony said: "Whoa! Big sucker, huh?" When I didn't answer, he lapsed back into silence.

We hit the highway into town above the valley where the land flattened out. I was looking forward to dropping Tony off and returning home—my mother's prayers had surely ended by now—but Tony grew more animated, looking out the side window, twisting in his seat. Suddenly he burst out: "Turn off. On the next gravel. Okay?"

I figured he had to piss, so I shrugged and turned right. The corn was already higher than the car. It flickered by, gray-green in the stray light. All the county roads had been surveyed in perfect grids, crisscrossing every mile, and the corn grew right up to the intersections, making them totally blind. Before we got close to the first one, I slowed down, thinking to let Tony out.

When I eased up on the gas, Tony, his voice low and tight, said: "No. Keep going." He gripped the dashboard.

I thought he'd never driven these gravel roads. "Can't," I said. "These intersections—you can't see around them. The corn."

Suddenly he slid over, pressed against me on the seat. His body was so hot it felt like a torpedo of warmth melting into me. He pressed me against the door, his shoulder hard on mine, our skin sticking together. Then his foot came down on mine, and the car surged forward as he floored the accelerator. The overpowered V-8 roared, and gravel sprayed from the rear tires.

"Jesus!" I yelled. Tony reached with his right hand through the spokes of the steering wheel, forcing me harder against the door, his hair against my cheek as I fought to control the fishtailing car. His foot pressed mine against the accelerator like an anvil. Light swung from cornfield to cornfield—and just like that, we were a hundred yards from the intersection, doing seventy miles an hour, struggling with each other. I tried to force him back, but I couldn't get leverage without moving the steering wheel and making the car veer violently. The door handle gouged my arm.

Then he shut off the lights.

Dark clapped in front of us. We rocketed through it toward the intersection. "Yeah," Tony whispered. Then the crossing opened and shut—that fast, on both sides of us—a snap of distance revealed and gone. The car heaved over the hump where the two roads met, slammed down on its shocks. Tony flung himself away from me.

I stopped the car, trembling so badly I could hardly hold the brake down. I slammed the transmission into park. "You dumb shit," I said quietly. He looked at me, his eyes black pits, a little starlight shine of sweat on his cheek. I braced myself with my left hand against the door and with my right I pushed him so hard that he slammed into the passenger door, his head thudding against the window. He bounced off as if he hadn't felt it. I pushed him a second time and was ready to do it again, envisioning him going through the door, when he said, "No, Robert."

I stopped with my hand on his shoulder. He had a peculiar habit of twisting his mouth—sort of the way a squirrel works a nut—and he did that now. Then he said: "Don't you see, Robert?"

"See?" I said. "You shut the lights off. Are you crazy?"

"If you shut your lights off," he said, "then if someone else's coming, you'll see *their* lights in the intersection."

I grunted, part disgust, part amazement. I took my hand from his shoulder, shook my head, and stared out the side window. Then I started to laugh.

"You see?" Tony asked. He smiled at me like he'd given me a gift and waited to know if I approved.

"Yeah, I see. You're one crazy bastard, Tony."

I put the car in drive. We looked at each other. I flicked on the lights. Then I stomped the accelerator down, and the car howled, surged forward, veering all over the road. "All *right*, Robert," Tony said, as if he were talking to himself.

By the time we came to the next intersection, we were doing seventy again. I cut the lights just before it, beheld nothing but darkness in the crossing. We shot through it and kept going. Through darkness after darkness after darkness.

We kept our friendship secret that summer. Tony's mother worked nights but stayed home weekends. She had two cars and kept the keys to both of them in her purse. Tony, however, had duplicated them, so on weekday evenings when she worked, he took whichever car she left. On weekends, however, he stayed shut up with her, while I visited with my usual friends and never said a word to them about him.

The corn grew up around us, higher, thicker and denser. The road crossings became more blind. Silence grew like algae between my mother and me. At meals I noticed the sound of silverware, and I'd catch her looking at me with that look that never led to speech. I felt that I was leaving her just as Dad had, and that she had no power to stop me. In my mind I almost dared her to. When I heard her begin the Rosary behind her bedroom door, I'd leave the house.

I'd find Tony cruising the streets. We'd cruise together for a while. Sometimes we'd drive the river bottom, sometimes we'd take the highway to Clear River. But no matter what else we did, at some point we'd go to the gravel roads. We'd drive ten or fifteen miles in a straight line, or we'd go to an unfamiliar part of the county and make turn after turn until we were lost, then line out in any direction at seventy or eighty miles an hour until we found a highway. In the intersections we'd sometimes see pale light, and we'd slam on the brakes, skidding and lurching toward it. And sometimes we wouldn't see light, but when we flashed through the crossing, we'd see headlights on the intersecting road. My heart would leap to my throat then, but the window of safety between the dark and light, though narrow, seemed certain.

In time, because of that certainty, I grew bored. There was always the chance that someone else approaching the intersection had his lights off too, but even this unlikely possibility lost its edge. One night I told Tony I'd grown tired of it.

"Wanna do it better?" he asked. He gazed at me, the green dashboard lights making his strange, wide-open eyes both reptilian and warm.

"How?" I asked.

"Take me back to my car."

He told me to follow him, and we drove a few miles out of town, turned off the highway, and parked at a gravel intersection where corn grew at all four corners. Tony got out of his car, came back, and stood beside my open window. The milky smell of corn pollen filled the humid breeze.

"This is it," Tony said, staring down the road. "I go straight ahead here and you turn right. Each goes to the next intersection and turns around. Then we come back to this one. When we get close, we turn our lights off or leave them on."

"Which one does what?" I asked.

"I don't know, Robert."

"But, Tony," I said. "Think. Don't you see . . . ?"

He turned his head slowly, met my eyes, and I realized that he *did* see. "Cornfield Roulette," he said.

I let that sink in. Tony's mouth moved in that little squirrel twitch. "It's a game, Robert," he said quietly.

"A game? Some game."

"I made it up," he said. "I've been thinking about it. What do *you* think, Robert? We're friends. What do you think?"

His quiet, his earnestness, infected me. My pulse knew I was going to say yes, but my mind still refused. "Tony," I said, "you shoulda stayed in that locker that time. They should never have let you out."

"I'll go straight, Robert," he said. He walked away from me, into my headlights. The summer wind blew his loose shirt out like wings.

"Tony!" I yelled.

He didn't stop.

"You're a dipshit, Tony."

He opened the door to his car, shut it, and started the engine. "Screw you, Tony," I yelled. I hit the gas and roared off the shoulder onto the road. I passed him in a cloud of dust and spraying gravel, jerked the wheel right at the intersection, and sped off. In my mirror I saw him cross behind me. I floored the car, feeling it force me back in the seat.

I didn't intend to play his game. I had a head start on him and a larger engine. It wouldn't take much—maybe only a second—to beat him through the intersection. He might think it a gamble, but I'd just make it a race. I spun the car around and floored it again, veering down the road as I headed back. The car straightened out, the carburetor howling as it sucked gas and air, the V-8 churning, the cornfields on both sides of me flickering like fences. I'd never driven this fast on gravel before. I was afraid to look at the speedometer, but I was going so fast the car seemed to hunker down, skidding over the surface of the road, far below the cliffs of corn.

I was scared but elated. My whole head throbbed. I wanted to be high up, to see it all, the two cars coming at right angles toward each other. I wanted to know where Tony was. But suddenly I had to make a decision. Lights on or off? I reached for the switch. My hand froze. I looked to the right, trying to see through the corn. Where was he?

"Damn!" I slammed the switch in. The intersection lay dark before me, and for the first time, that darkness terrified me. It might mean he was there, but it was too late to stop. I rocketed into the gap, flying over the hump where the two roads met. As I flew through, I glanced to the right and cheered in relief and victory. Tony's headlights consumed the road, but he wasn't close enough for them to show in the intersection.

"Cornfield Roulette, Tony?" I yelled, watching him shoot through the crossing in the mirror. "Yeah, I'll play your Cornfield Roulette." I slammed on the brakes, stopped the car in a skidding explosion of gravel, did a three-point on the road and drove back to the intersection. I turned in Tony's direction, flashed my lights on and off, and got out of the car.

I wasn't as calm as I pretended. My knees trembled, and I held on to the door. I felt as if I had a fever. Tony drove up slowly and stopped beside me, rolled his window down. His headlights radiated long streaks in my vision, and his face seemed to float in the darkness framed by his window.

"That sure was fun, Tony," I said. "You got any more games you've thought up?"

"You can't just play it once," he said. His voice was truly calm, as if stating a known fact.

"What the hell do you mean by that?" I asked.

"You're supposed to keep going, Robert," he said. "Through the intersection down to the next one turn around come back, through, back. Like that."

"And how many times are you supposed to do this? Till you run outta gas?"

"Four."

Nothing could have surprised me more—he had an actual number! "Four?" I asked. "Why the hell *four*?"

"Odds," he said. "There's four possibilities. Lights on and on, off and off, on and off, and off and on. You gotta do it four times for the odds. Otherwise there's no winning."

"Staying alive's winning," I said.

"Only if you beat the odds. Three more. Okay, Robert?"

I was angry now—at myself for not just walking away from this, and at him for not dropping it. "Okay," I said. "Three more. But that's it."

"That's it," he said.

I got in my car, made the turn, and headed down the road again—more than ever determined not to play the game. Because of the turn, he had a head start on me, but I was calmer this time, and I intended to blow him off the road. I'd seen how much faster my car was, and I drove now as if possessed. I decided to shut my lights off again, doing one of those he'll-think-I'll-do-this-so-I'll-do-that mental kind of thing as I drove. But I didn't think it'd matter. I cookied the turn and poured back down the road, cutting the lights a hundred yards from the intersection.

At thirty yards I saw Tony's lights, the faintest shimmer on the road. But rather than stopping, I kept the engine floored, grim now, determined to beat him through, to destroy this game he was somehow forcing me to play. The light grew before me, but I blasted through, blinded when I looked to the right, the whole interior of the car illuminated. I grinned, though my lips stuck to my teeth, and I held my middle finger up into the light.

Both times my speed had carried me. "Screw your game, Tony," I muttered. The third time I left my lights on, and

Tony did too—but his were farther down the road. I was gaining on him. One more time. I spun the car around at the intersection, hit the gas, and swayed back toward the crossing point.

I felt calm now, though I think, looking back, that it was the numbness of rage and fear burned to ash. Tony had frightened me, terrified me, and I couldn't admit it. I wanted to humiliate him. I had one grim focus: to pass through the intersection so far ahead of him he'd feel ashamed of the crate he was driving, ashamed to have thought up this game. I wanted to make fun of him afterward. I wanted to rub it in until he turned his face from me.

I roared down the road between the cornfields as thick, hot air poured through the windows. The roll of frogs and the frantic chirp of crickets seemed to come from far away. I saw the road in my headlights like a wire down which I spun. Nothing else mattered. I felt collected, balanced within dust and sweat and speed. The intersection seemed to rise before me. I left my lights on, no longer caring what Tony might do.

I shot from the blinding corn, and suddenly, as if it emerged from a hole in the air, Tony's car was on top of me. It seemed to lurch from nowhere, then glide with impossible speed. Everything seemed made of grease and dark oil, and he and I were sliding in it, swaying and floating toward each other. I heard the faraway crickets and frogs. Everything was too fast and too slow. It seemed like a dance, a waltz. We shifted, spun, balanced, spiraled into a center. I saw Tony's face, a calm white mask behind his windshield, his eyes wide open. They contained neither terror nor surprise. They seemed to look into mine but not see me at all.

I was a fraction of a second ahead of him and going faster. I didn't have time to take my foot off the gas. If I had slowed down at all—if I'd seen him sooner, even if I'd been prepared to stop, or if I'd been expecting him—both of us would have died. But my knee was locked, the accelerator jammed to the floor. Tony's car loomed huge as I passed in front of it. My side window couldn't contain it.

I rose on the hump of the intersection, felt my tires leave the earth. I floated for eternity before the car whumped on its shocks. Cornfields swayed crazily on either side of the zigzagging road, golden pollen spraying out of the tassels into my lights, a golden rain rising upward in the wind. It streamed before me as I blundered through it, fighting for control—a rain of stars from the edge of nowhere, blinding and blessing me.

Then I was stopped, a half mile from the intersection, staring into the empty space my headlights exposed. I shut them off, flung open the door, and stumbled out into the road ditch. Needing to feel something alive, I sank into the grass, grasping its rough, cool surfaces. I stared into the dark sweet-corn field, unable to believe what had almost happened. He couldn't have missed me by more than inches.

I heard his car come up and stop, but I didn't turn around. He sank down beside me in silence. I couldn't look at him, didn't even have the strength for anger or revulsion. After a moment he reached out and plucked a grass blade and began to rip it into narrow strips. Then he rolled it all into a ball and flung it toward the cornfield.

"You won, Robert," he said. "Beat the odds."

I put my head in my hands. I didn't trust my voice. I didn't trust him, didn't trust myself. It sank into me what had happened. He had turned around sooner to make up for my speed, estimating from the other runs where he had to turn. But worse than that, I realized what it meant that I had seen his face through the windshield. His lights had been off. Mine were on. He *knew* I was there.

A hollow crucifix hangs on my mother's wall. Made of blond, polished wood, it slides open like a pencil box. Inside are two small beeswax candles, a little bottle of holy water, and some matches. A slit in the top of the base allows you to insert the cover, the flat cross with Jesus hanging on it, so that it stands upright. Two holes in the base, right under where Jesus' wrists are nailed, provide candle holders. Light the candles, and you have an immediate shrine.

Mom told me when I was young that this crucifix was meant for emergencies. If someone was dying and beyond the reach of a priest, the holy water and candles would suffice. She'd never let me open the holy water or light the candles— they had to be saved. As it turned out, we didn't even think of using this crucifix when my father died. As soon as I told Mom how he was staring at the sky, she put him in the car and took him straight to the hospital. I wasn't there when a priest administered the last rites.

My parents hung their rosaries on this hollow crucifix and took them down on Friday nights. Dad's rosary was made of wooden beads, Mom's of blue-green glass with a silver cross and chain. I hated Friday-night Rosaries when Dad was alive. After he died, Mom no longer forced me to participate, though she said the Rosary herself every night.

When I turned in my driveway after leaving Tony, I saw

a light in the kitchen window. Usually my mother went to bed early; my heart sank. She would ask me what I'd been doing, and I'd have to lie.

When I entered the back door, I heard the murmur of prayers, the singsongy rise and fall of the Hail Marys. I shut my eyes and leaned against the door. I waited through four Hail Marys, the sound like rain in the house, until she came to the end of the decade. I heard her name it: "The fourth Glorious Mystery: the Crowning of the Virgin Mary as Queen of Heaven." She still had two decades to go. I couldn't wait that long. And I knew that if she was on the Glorious Mysteries, she was doing them all, since on Wednesdays she usually said the Sorrowful. That meant she'd been through the Joyful, the Sorrowful, and part of the Glorious already, the entire cycle of the Rosary.

I pushed myself away from the door and walked into the bright kitchen. I had to go through the living room to get to bed. I expected her to break the prayer, but she didn't, not even when the kitchen floor creaked under me. I looked carefully in at her. She sat in a far corner under the sliding crucifix, upright in a chair, her feet flat on the floor. In the dim light I saw her fingers move on the beads as she started another Hail Mary. Light flowed for an instant in the blue-green glass. Her eyes were closed.

It was only two steps to the stairway door. I almost took them, but her voice, alone, stopped me. It didn't contain my father's, and I realized that was why I couldn't stand to hear her praying. Her prayers were rich and musical, but they didn't fill the room as they had when Dad's blended with them. I watched her fingers move again, watched the rosary she held ripple in her hands, then fall still as the prayer began.

I walked silently across the carpet. I reached up and took Dad's rosary off the crucifix. The wooden beads clacked softly as I enclosed them in my hand. I sat down on the couch. Mom never stopped praying. I saw where she was in the decade, placed my forefinger and thumb on the right bead.

I opened my mouth to join her, but I couldn't speak. I couldn't give voice to the prayers, so I just moved my fingers on the beads that my father's fingers had worn smooth, had polished until they felt like warm, quiet stone. I wondered if this was Dad's whole life, to have worn a rosary smooth. And I wondered if it was enough. And I thought that prayer is like water. It wears smooth the world.

When the Rosary was finished, Mom kissed the silver cross, then folded the beads into her palm. She opened her eyes and looked at me. I thought it would be the look that I dreaded, and for a moment it was, but then it broke into words. "Thank God you're safe," she said. "If something would happen to you, Bobbie, I don't think I could stand it."

I watched Dad's rosary collapse into my hand. It felt to me as if his life were collapsing there, a soul of wood and stone. I held it, then looked back up at my mother. Her eyes no longer appeared helpless to me. It's only now that I understand my relief.

I don't know how she knew or what she knew, but she'd risen from bed and prayed fifteen decades of the Rosary, alone. She must have started about the time that Tony stood outside my car window explaining Cornfield Roulette.

"I know, Mom," I said. "I know. Nothing'll happen to me."

For the rest of that summer I fed the cattle, painted the

granary, read or watched television in the evenings, or walked in the frog-filled night. Mom and I sometimes remembered Dad together. We found we could do that. On weekends, when I knew Tony wouldn't be out, I drove to town and saw my old friends. I never went on weekdays, and I didn't talk to anyone about what Tony and I had done. I wanted to forget his white face, his staring eyes behind the windshield, and his car sliding out of the dark.

In late summer, just before school started, the red-tailed hawks gathered in the thermals rising off the hot land, circling over alfalfa and oat stubble. I looked up from doing afternoon chores one day and saw four of them high above me, hardly more than specks. I opened my mouth to call to Dad in the feed wagon but stopped, half turned around, remembering that he wasn't there.

Then, one Saturday in early September when I was grinding corn, swinging a scoopful into the auger of the hammer mill, I saw Tony watching me. He stood unmoving next to the tractor, in the hot blast from its radiator fan, his untucked shirt snapping. I jerked in alarm but hid the movement in the swing of the shovel. The noise of the hammer mill had concealed his arrival. He'd come like an apparition. I paused for a moment and looked at him. His mouth moved. I returned to the corn I was shoveling.

He watched me until the hammer mill tank was full. I went to the tractor, throttled it down, considered just driving away. Then I shut it off.

"Hello, Tony," I said.

He moved two steps closer, so that he stood right at the rear wheel of the tractor, and looked up at me. "My dad's home, Robert," he said.

We'd never spoken of the fact that his father didn't live with him, and his words surprised me, but I didn't show it. "Well, good," I said.

"Only for a week."

I nodded. "A week's a week," I said. "I got work, Tony. Gotta unload this feed."

He didn't move away from the rear wheel. "Sure, Robert," he said. His mouth twitched again. "He brought me a gun. You want to see it?"

I started the tractor, looked through the blue diesel smoke at the horizon. I didn't want to see his gun. I'd been shooting guns for years, and it didn't interest me. I wanted Tony to leave, but I couldn't resist his helplessness. He seemed completely self-sufficient, withdrawn into himself, and yet totally dependent on me in some way.

I looked down at him. "Okay," I said. "I've gotta unload this feed first. Climb on." I nodded at the tractor hitch. He stood there, holding onto the seat, while I drove to the feed wagon. He watched while I unloaded the hammer mill and shut the tractor off. Then we walked to the yard. He'd driven over in a pickup—his father's, I assumed. Tony pulled a high-powered rifle with a scope attached out from behind the seat and handed it to me.

"What do you think, Robert?"

"Real nice," I said, hefting it.

"A .243 Winchester," he said. "For deer."

"Yeah. Your dad gave it to you, huh?"

"Yeah. You want to shoot it?"

"I don't know. I got to feed the cattle."

"C'mon, Robert. I can't shoot it in town."

"Goddamn, Tony!" I was sick of his suggestions, his quiet pressure. "What do you think, I—"

His eyes stopped me. Until now they had always been unreadable blanks, taking something in that no one else could see, but they were suddenly luminous with tears. I looked over my shoulder at the cattle yard so he wouldn't see that I'd seen.

"What the hell," I said. "I can feed the cattle later."

We walked up the field road. I held the rifle back out to him. "Here," I said. "Find a dirt clod."

"You shoot it first," he said.

"It's your gun. Go ahead and shoot it."

"I want *you* to have the first shot," he said.

He meant it as a gift, but I almost threw the weapon down and grabbed him. *What the hell is he doing?—he tries to kill me and then expects me to be grateful for the honor of shooting the damn gun first?* I felt like mashing his skinny body worse than Nate or Meryl ever had, forcing out of him whatever in God's name he'd been thinking that night.

I stared down at the Winchester in my hands, feeling trapped. Why was it that the only thing ever clear to me with Tony around was my own confusion? "Okay," I said finally, giving in again. "Is it sighted in?"

I hated his little smile of gratitude. "Yeah. Dad did it before he gave it to me."

I picked out a clump of dirt about fifty yards up the road and took the shot hurriedly, standing up, the crosshairs wavering. I squeezed the trigger, the rifle bucked, and when I looked again, the clump had disappeared.

"All *right*, Robert," Tony said beside me.

When I handed the gun back, he asked: "What do you think, Robert?"

Why do you care what I think? I wanted to say. *Why the hell do you care?* Instead, I said: "It's real good."

"It is, isn't it?"

He held the rifle carelessly, letting the barrel swing as we walked. I'd clicked on the safety before I gave it back, but nevertheless I avoided the swinging barrel. We walked a long way before I said: "You gonna shoot?"

"I want something real."

"We're not going to find anything. The crops're up."

"Just a little farther."

We were at least a quarter mile from the house, and I wanted to get back, but I walked on with him, the fields buzzing with insects, the corn leaves clattering. Then Tony stopped.

"There," he said, pointing to a dead cottonwood that rose from the fence line, two hundred yards away. On its very top, the dark, squatting shape of a hawk carved a small hole in the blue sky.

"No," I said.

But Tony moved to a wooden fence post and placed the barrel on it. His father must have taught him how to shoot. He clicked the safety off. I walked over and placed my hand over the scope. Tony pulled his eye away from it and looked into my face.

"What are you doing, Robert?" he asked.

"Stopping you," I said.

"It's just a hawk."

"We don't shoot hawks on this farm."

A long moment passed. His mouth twitched, and he

looked from me to the hawk, then back again. His eyes narrowed and blazed—for a moment I thought he might strike me—then he looked at the distant hawk again.

"Goddamn," he said as quietly as a hissing fuse. "Why is someone always in my way?"

"Anything else, Tony," I said.

"Even you. Why are you in my way, Robert?"

"We don't shoot hawks here."

His mouth worked. I might have laughed, but the situation was too tense. His mouth worked and worked, like he was chewing all around something. Finally, in a voice that seemed to leak from him, he said: "I want to shoot it, Robert. I really *want* to."

I was prepared for anything but honesty—the simple want, without excuses, apologies, or explanation. Had he appealed to anything but his own desire, I would have held firm. But for the first time since I'd met him, I felt him speak a whole truth. I'd never heard anyone say that they wanted to kill a hawk—wanted to kill anything—in the flat, open way that Tony said it. Always there was some other reason— to protect chickens or crops, to eat, as a natural result of the hunt—always some reason outside the human heart. Tony showed me a part of his heart. Had I looked long enough, maybe I would have seen its cruel convolutions, its senselessness. But his voice expressed the hope that I wouldn't look too long, that I'd understand what he himself didn't. It broke me. It shouldn't have, but it did.

I looked at the hawk, needing excuses myself. It was two hundred yards away—he'd never hit it. That rifle could, but the odds were against it.

"All right," I said. "I'll let you try."

"Thanks, Robert," he said.

He was going to say more, but intimacy, especially unasked for, does not necessarily make us kind. "Shoot if you're going to, goddammmit," I said. "I got things to do."

His eyes darkened. He turned, laid the rifle back on the post, sighted. I watched the distant, huddled shape. Tony shuffled his feet. A dust devil ran down the soybean field, twisting the vines.

The shot boomed. "Jesus!" Tony yelled, staggering back.

The hawk rose off the tree. Its wings opened wide. It stroked the air, once, twice. Then the rhythm of its wings shattered, and it tumbled straight down.

"I did it," Tony said. I'd never heard awe in his voice before.

I didn't say anything. I climbed over the fence and began to walk through the soybeans toward the tree. Behind me, I heard Tony climbing the fence, struggling with the rifle. I ran, the soybeans catching at my feet. I didn't want him walking with me, but I heard him trying to catch up. I stopped short and turned around.

"Don't run!" I shouted. "Don't you ever run with a gun in your hands, Tony! What are you, a dumbshit? Walk! Put that thing on safe, and don't swing it around like a damn stick. Didn't your father teach you anything?"

I strode away, but I couldn't contain my fury and turned back. He stared at me, his mouth working, the rifle held across his body.

"And don't you dare fall down, Tony!" I shouted. Then, because I was afraid that if I faced him any longer, I'd rush to him and beat him senseless, I ran from him again, toward the hawk.

The bird lay a few yards away from the tree, along the fence line. Its wings, skewed wide, floated on the grass. It had no head—an impossibly lucky shot. Actually, he'd missed, aimed at the bird's body and hit its head. Its nerves alone had lifted it from the tree, commanded it hopelessly to seek air and height.

I knelt beside it. Blood stained the neck feathers, raw bone and muscle protruding from the stump. I folded its wings into its body, stroked the smooth breast. When Tony came up, I didn't look at him.

"It's a bad deal, Tony," I finally said.

I lifted the bird up against my chest and stood. A claw scratched my wrist.

"It is, Robert?"

"A real bad deal," I said.

"What are you going to do?"

I walked away.

"Why not leave it?"

"I don't know," I said. "Shut up, Tony. Just shut up."

We walked wordlessly down the field road. I went ahead, cradling the hawk, Tony lagging behind with the rifle. I heard his footsteps stop and was about to turn around, a wave of apprehension filling me, when I heard a crash and the sound of glass breaking. I spun. Tony stood near a crooked fence post, the Winchester raised over his head, the scope skewed in its mountings, crushed on one end. The gun was already arcing down again when he felt my eyes and somehow stopped it. Trembling, he slowly lowered the weapon until it angled across his chest, and he stood for a moment like a caricature of a soldier. His mouth twitched.

Then he marched past me in silence, little puffs of dust rising from his torn sneakers, his eyes fixed on the horizon. Stroking the hawk's breast, I stared at a glitter of refracted light in the grass near the post. By the time I turned around, Tony was a thin, ragged figure, erect, passing behind the corn where the field road curved.

I followed him back, but his pickup was gone when I got there, and we never spoke again. I placed the dead hawk in the granary, then finished chores. Later I stood in the granary for a long time, staring at the bird; it was already turning gray and dusty. Finally I went to the house, crept into the living room and removed the hollow crucifix from the wall, placing my mother's rosary on an end table and putting my father's in my pocket. I carried the crucifix back to the granary and set the covering cross upright in the stand, next to the body of the hawk. Trying to handle them as I thought a priest would, I inserted the smooth, tapered candles into the base and lit the clean wicks.

With the holy water I wet the hawk's neck feathers and slowly rubbed them one by one, but the blood only faded, wouldn't wash out. I reached into my pocket and took out the wooden rosary. I thought of Tony, of my father staring at the sky, of the dead hawk's leap into the air—none of which I understood but all of which hovered, calling for prayer in the silence around me. I held the rosary's small cross between my thumb and forefinger, but got only as far as the "I believe" of the Apostle's Creed before choking.

For the first time, I truly understood that my father was gone. He was gone, and part of his absence I'd have to bear on my own. Did I really *have* to betray him to understand that? It all seemed so needless, yet so necessary. I knelt in the granary, my sobs smothered by dust and wood, my fingers running back and forth over the beads Dad's hands had worn so smooth. I might have let myself kneel there and weep until I was exhausted and spent, the candle flames coronas through my tears, if I hadn't remembered that soon Mom would expect me in for supper.

I wiped my tears on my sleeve and gathered myself, then plucked one of the hawk's tail feathers and moved it nearer the beeswax candles, turning it to catch the faint red tinge. Suddenly it caught fire and—for an instant—glowed a bright, translucent red before shriveling into bitter smoke. I breathed it in, and rose.

A Strange Brown Fruit

I think I am a gentle man. I do not boast: I mean nothing more than that I am unlikely to blow away a neighbor as he mows his lawn, or to engage in car bombings in congested areas. I cannot prove this. It is only a faith I have, and any day it could be shaken. I could fall into a terrible rage and do horrid, ungentle things. But I have faith that I will not—partly, I must admit, because I am infirm now and well along in life, but more for other reasons.

There was this rabbit, you see, when I was just a boy. I don't quite know why it became my responsibility. By chance, I suppose, because I was the one who found it. It's strange that the great weight of responsibility, even for life and death, should be assigned by chance. Yet often that's the way it happens. You open the door and find a starving kitten freezing on the stoop in a cold winter, and suddenly you're responsible for it. Someone else might have opened the door, your wife or your husband, and you could have gone on watching your soap opera or reading the newspaper, dispassionate at the news of another murder, another bombing, another capsule of cyanide found in an aspirin bottle.

But it was you who opened the door, perhaps to check the weather or to leave for work, or to bring in wood for the fireplace. It might have been another moment, and the kitten might have gone, but instead there it is, and you're responsible for it. Do you think you can simply step over it, go to work or collect your wood or note the condition of the weather and step back inside? No. Your whole day has changed. Only one who loves you greatly will take that responsibility from you.

My mother loved me, but she didn't volunteer. I left the rabbit lying on the porch, on the warm cement, and opened the screen door with my left hand because my right hand had blood on it from carrying the thing. It was a baby rabbit, and it lay without moving, its eyes unblinking and one torn ear limp along its back. Its breathing was so fast that it vibrated on the cement. It waxed and waned in the wind and summer smells.

I called into the dark, cool kitchen. Had my father been around, I might have sought him out, he being the one who normally handled and delivered death on our farm. But he was gone, somewhere in the landscape, lost behind the bulk and curve of earth, on which were stuck the plants that gave us our living. I was a lonely child, I suppose, among all this, wandering the space of the farm, miles from town, without siblings. But that's beside the point. Who, upon enough reflection, wouldn't make a similar claim to childhood loneliness?

The hydraulic piston on the screen door whooshed and pumped, whooshed and pumped. My voice touched the metal pans, rang among them, ran into the living room, curled upstairs and sank down the basement steps and faded. The screen door slammed with a rattle of chains and left only the buzzing of the refrigerator—empty rooms, and life holding on or maybe not holding on, maybe waning more than it waxed, but vibrating, shining there on the dusty cement where I'd left it. I called again, louder, and my mother answered from back by the washer.

"Come here," I called. "I want to show you something."

I heard movement, back and forth steps, water running. Finally she appeared in the kitchen, her face white with weariness and soap dust, her abrupt cheekbones shining in the light, shining as if the bones were pushing their way through the tissue and skin. There were times when my mother seemed inconceivably old to me, like something weathered and still, something lying in the open. No doubt my own face now begins to give a similar impression. In the mirror, I can't see it, but in my unrehearsed expressions, others might.

"What is it?" my mother asked, coming toward me across the kitchen, her hands in the pockets of her faded housecoat.

I couldn't talk. I merely pointed through the screen. She came and stood over me, smelling of soap and bleach.

"You've got blood on your hand."

I'd been staring at the rabbit, and her words startled me. They were a statement, without emotion. I realized that my finger was still outstretched, and glistening wet and red in the awl-like light of summer and midday into which I had thrust it. I let my hand drop to my side, out of the light. I didn't know what to do with it, wanted to shove it into my pocket, but was afraid to get blood on my pants.

"I carried it up here," I said in explanation.

"Where'd you find it?"

"By Rodney's dish."

"Damn dog. Why didn't he just kill it?"

She was less excited than I wanted her to be. Not excited at all, in fact. Her hands were still inside her housecoat, and she stood just at the edge of the square of light coming though the door, erect, not even bending into it to get a better look.

A breeze ruffled the rabbit's fur. Beneath the parted fur I could see skin so delicate and white it seemed translucent, as if glazed with milk. The blood had stopped flowing, but the marks of Rodney's teeth were deep and vile, the rabbit's neck and shoulder torn.

"Do you think it's going to live?"

"No."

The word was too quick, too short and definite. And without emotion.

"But you haven't even looked," I cried, turning and staring up into her face.

She looked back at me. Her right hand came out from her housecoat and rested on my head. But her voice remained the same. "Some things don't need closer looking, son. Some things just don't."

"But what are we going to do?" I was on the verge of whining, and I knew she hated that.

"You'll have to kill it. Can't just leave it suffer there."

I stared through the screen door, not at the rabbit but at the cornfield beyond, the straight green lines diminishing toward the blue sky. It was an understood rule in our family that any animal wounded beyond hope must be killed. If my father hit a bird with a car, he always made sure that the bird was dead. Once, even, late for church, and dressed in his Sunday best, he'd chased a wounded-winged bird into a patch of sand burrs. My mother didn't protest when he returned to the car, but quietly picked burrs out of his coat and pants all the way into town and then waited in the vestibule of the church while he went to the restroom to wash.

But I'd been ready to protest this time, to insist that the rabbit not be killed. Then she said: "You," and there was nothing I could say. I couldn't protest to myself, and I couldn't ask her to do it for me, and then protest that she shouldn't. And I couldn't protest the rule itself. I didn't have the arguments then. I don't have them now.

The refrigerator stopped running. The house rang in its noiselessness. Against the sky a barn swallow reached the top of its arc, stopped, tipped, swooped down, beat its wings in a flutter.

"The sooner the better," my mother said. "Then come back and wash your hands."

Still staring through the screen, not looking at her, I felt her hand lift from my head, then heard her footsteps recede across the kitchen floor, then, a bit later, the squeak of rollers on the washer, and a cabinet door being opened and shut— her life already, so soon, ordinary again.

The rabbit vibrated. It had closed its eyes since I laid it down, and it seemed even smaller now, a pathetic, small vibration. I reached for the latch on the screen door, saw my red, pointed finger, clawed to grasp the latch, burst bright in the hard light. I dropped it again to my side and opened the latch with my left hand. The door swung out over the rabbit, grazed its ear, whooshed and pumped, grazed its ear again, slammed shut. I stood over the animal. It didn't move.

As gently as I could, I slid my right hand under it and picked it up. Its fur was still damp from Rodney's saliva. Its bright eyes popped open, as bright and hard as the light itself, and without surface. I carried it chest-high, facing away from me. Near the edge of the trees that formed our windbreak stood a row of dusty grain bins, tall burning weeds and catnip growing up around them. I went behind one of these bins, disappearing completely in the weeds, and set the rabbit down on an old stump rotting in the middle. I set it down where the wood was firm, on the outside perimeter.

When I was very young, I used to dance with glee when my father killed chickens. I hated picking off the feathers and butchering, but I loved the killing. He would hold the chicken in one hand, lay its neck on a block, grip an ax halfway down the handle with his other hand, lift it, drop it, fling the body, spattering blood, away from him onto the grass. Headless, the body would thrust with its legs, hopping on the grass, turn somersaults, half fly, beat the air and ground. I'd dance with these bodies. Such careless movement.

Again and again I asked my father to let me handle the ax. Year after year he refused. Then one year he handed it to me. I wasn't very old, in early grade school yet. I gripped the ax, reached into the wire cage, pulled a chicken out by its legs. I took it to the brown-stained block and adjusted it carefully. It kept curling its neck, looking at me with one eye. I twisted it to straighten the neck, and it only curled it again. Finally I managed to get it a little straighter, and I raised the ax. It came up heavy and too slow. The neck began to curl.

I forced the ax down, but I had too little power; it was ponderous, full of inertia, not to be hurried. The one eye gazed at me, and the bright, bitter blade came down, falling of its own accord, beyond my control.

The neck curled away, and the ax only grazed it. Blood appeared, but the head remained attached. The bird squawked, jumped in my hand. I raised the ax again, in something like a panic, and the cries of the bird, horrid, ancient, and reptilian, went flinging out about the farm, an accusation of the awful things being committed. The other chickens huddled in the cage. The cries came back from the buildings. The ax came down, and I flung the body, the fat, stupid, useless body, away from me, not watching it but hearing the irregular beat of wings, the velvet feathers against the grass—a betrayal of flight. The head lay on the block, and I stared at it, bent over, my hand still gripping the ax. The eye blinked once, and it seemed puzzled, nothing more—not angry or afraid—just puzzled at so great an absence. Then it shut, and the comb turned gray, and it seemed to me horrid that so much of a chicken was body.

You may say my father was cruel, to give me the ax when I didn't have the power it required. Well, perhaps he didn't know. Or perhaps he did. In any case, it became my duty after that, every time we butchered chickens, to take the ax at least once, and I learned to power it, I learned the movements and muscles required to take those lives. Glee was gone, and dancing. It was a lesson in gentleness. Had I had more power, it might have been the reverse.

But a chicken, after all, is hard to love. A rabbit—a baby rabbit—is another thing. It lay there on the stump, its eyes shut, waiting. I wished I hadn't found it. I wished it had gone on suffering, as long as I didn't know, as long as its suffering made no demands on me. I hated Rodney.

And I had nothing with which to kill it. The problem of finding something dazed me, left me uncomprehending. As long as my hands were empty, there was a certain gap between this moment and the moment of the rabbit's death. But once I chose a tool and held it in my hands, time would begin to hurry, to flicker like a wheel. I might have simply picked the rabbit up by its hind legs and dashed its head against the stump. (One hates to even imagine it! Why is that? Would it not have been the speediest thing, the kindest?) That thought, however, was beyond me.

I cast about in the weeds, kicking them over with my boots. Junk lay among them: bits of tin and sheet metal, baling wire, twine. I passed over them all and finally chose a metal bar, two feet long, a half inch in diameter. I picked this bar out of the weeds, hefted it, felt a pleasing kind of weight, a momentum and mass, as I swung it slowly, moving my wrist.

So I stood over the rabbit with this, and time did flicker like a wheel until it seemed to be running slowly backward even as it raced forward, and I imagined the sound this bar would make when it met the animal's skull. I almost heard the sound.

And I dropped the bar. Actually, I threw it far from me, back into the weeds. It hit an empty grain bin, and clatter upon clatter went up, ringing in the summer air. I felt sick with the sound I'd imagined, and with desperation: How could I possibly do what I had to do, what my mother and even I expected me to do? I looked about me again, but there were no answers lying in the junk at the base of the weeds.

And suffering continued before my eyes, so much suffering contained in such small space.

Suddenly I turned and bolted for the house, relieved with a thought that flashed upon me. I burst into the dim kitchen and up the stairs, stumbling through the growing heat, the closeness of the upper hall. In my room I checked the top of my dresser, the table where I studied during the school year, the shelves where I kept my stamp collection. Finally, in the closet, I found what I was looking for—a slingshot made of a Y-shaped branch, powered with strips of inner tube, with a piece of leather for a pouch. I clambered back down the stairs with this in my hand. In the kitchen my mother watched me, her face pure and white and questioning, but I slammed through the screen door without stopping and pounded, gasping, across the lawn.

My hand searched for stones in the gravel of the driveway and found three of them—smooth, round stones, warm, sun-soaked stones. Two I thrust into my pocket. The third I fitted into the leather pouch of the slingshot as I ran back toward the grove and the grain bins and the weeds.

The rabbit lay where I'd left it, eyes shut. Sweat burned my eyes. With my forearm I wiped it out, clumsily, holding the slingshot with both hands. My running in and out had created a narrow path in the weeds; hurriedly I widened this, kicking the weeds down. It would have been faster to knock them down with one of the sticks or pieces of metal lying about, but now that I had the slingshot in my hands, and the stone fitted, I couldn't let it go.

Finally I stopped, dirty and itching, and caught my breath. I had knocked a sightway through the weeds far enough back from the rabbit. A wind came through the weeds and chilled my brow. It must have moved the rabbit's fur, but standing where I was, I couldn't tell. I sighted through the V of the slingshot, down through the corridor of ragged green, the broken stems whose juices stained my boots. I brought the stone back to my cheek, felt the power of my arms tighten in the straps, far more power than I needed to take so weak a life.

Holding on, holding on, I waited for the wind to die. I was good with a slingshot. I was very good. The heatless sun lay on my head. The weeds stopped moving. Something was terribly wrong in all I was doing, but I didn't know what. The leather slipped from my fingers, and the stone caught friction from the air and disappeared down its sure, receding trajectory as if sucked into the rabbit. The sound of the sudden meeting, far away, was lost in the careless snap of rubber straps recoiling. Far away from me, down a corridor of green, something soft and brown was pushed to the middle of a rotten stump by something fast and hard.

It takes years to repent for old mistakes. Just recently, taking a walk, I saw a pigeon hit by a car. The pigeon fluttered in the street as the driver continued on behind his tons of metal. I paused, but then, though aged enough to be a bit infirm, I hobbled after the bird. It took me quite a chase to catch it, for a pigeon, even broken-winged, has a lightness of body that a man can never know. It stayed beyond my reach for a long time, but finally I caught it. I wasted no time, and only, I think, the smallest bit of power. I felt its bones between my fingers—oh, if you could feel them, such wonderful, beautiful bones, the hollow, architectural bones of a bird, full of air and delicate strength.

I snapped them, with two fingers.

Such gentleness is difficult. I learned it from that rabbit. For I had to touch it in the end, and I walked down that corridor of broken and failing weeds with the juice of guilt inside me. I picked up the piece of flesh, held it at arm's length, my elbow straight, flung it like a grenade deep into the grove. At the top of its arc it hit a branch and hung there, sagging, a strange brown fruit. I gazed at it, dismayed. It seemed a vile mistake grown by the tree, an awful thing if plucked. I followed my pathway back out of the weeds. On the driveway I reached into my pocket and dropped the two leftover stones. The blood on my hand had turned dry and brown, and my pants remained unstained.

I went to my room and returned the slingshot to my closet before going to the bathroom to wash my hands. I had to go through the kitchen and laundry room to reach the bathroom, and I walked erectly, though it made no difference, for my mother had her back to me, sorting clothes. I shut the bathroom door and turned on the faucet. All businesslike, I scrubbed at the blood, and it dissolved in the clear, pure water. I was toweling my hands when there was a knock on the door.

"Come in."

My mother entered. She stood behind me. I continued to dry my hands, running the towel down between my fingers, keeping busy. I looked into the mirror and saw her face, so white, so indescribably old, her cheekbones pushing through to catch the light, to cup it and cast it back—a glistening, translucent surface tightened by the bones.

"It's not easy," she said.

I looked down and folded the towel, folded it again, making sure the corners met. I hung it up, wrapped it over the bar so that it was perfectly even. My eyes were burning. I shook my head. I felt my mother's hand on my hair: five fingers and a palm, bones contained in flesh. I turned and ducked under her, left her standing there, watching her own reflection.

The Heart of the Sky

IT surprised even me when Lennis Wagner filled in his tile
intake and let the slough he'd drained re-form. To go out
with a shovel and sledgehammer and smash the tile intake,
after spending all that money putting it in and getting good
crops off the reclaimed land, and to fill the intake up with
dirt—at first I didn't believe it, quite, even though Lennis
himself told me he'd done it. Like everyone else, I waited for
the proof. It took two years to come—cattails reasserting
themselves, and finally the red-winged and yellow-headed
blackbirds waving on the ends of reeds chirruping, and the
sound of frogs rolling across the fields clear to my place in
the evenings.

I've been good friends with Lennis since high school, and
we still work together, but it took him a long time to tell me
what had happened—chinks of talk filling in the spaces between work. It was obvious enough to everyone when

Adrian became pregnant, but no one ever thought to connect that to Lennis taking a hammer to his tile.

He and Mary were sitting in their living room one evening before going to bed. Lennis has even told me what he was reading—a *Successful Farming* magazine—and Mary was doing a crossword puzzle, when Adrian came downstairs. Lennis glanced up from his magazine and saw the expression on her face, and, he says, knew right then what she was going to say. He was on his feet and moving toward her before she'd finished with, 'Dad. Mom. I have to talk to you.'

Adrian used to hover around her father while he worked, and he'd stop to answer her questions, put up with her attempts to help. Mary was more demanding, less close to her daughter. Small enough, even healthy, differences, I suppose—differences a family can ignore. But crises magnify such differences. By the time Adrian spoke her next words, her father had her in his arms, while Mary was still sitting in her chair.

It's not hard to see how things can set and harden in an instant. Years of a family living within its tensions carefully, keeping them from congealing, flexible, like moving in molasses—and then, like that, everything is set.

There was Mary, watching.

'You're pregnant.' She repeated Adrian's words. A statement. With accusation inside it. The only available option, really, with Lennis having preempted sympathy and understanding. And stared at her husband and daughter with a face collapsed like a balloon losing air.

She couldn't see what Lennis himself felt. He told me he felt like throwing Adrian from him. "My own daughter, Charlie," he said. "You know what that feels like? I wanted to throw her down and then find the punk she met at the damn canning factory and pound him. That's what I really wanted to do.''

But he's not the kind of man to let his emotions get out of control. He kept his arms around Adrian. Told himself what's done is done.

Of course Mary couldn't see that. She looked at Adrian held in her father's arms and said dryly, 'Well, Adrian, I am disappointed. I thought you knew better.'

Adrian had been sobbing, but at her mother's words she stopped. She brought her face up from her father's chest. 'I'm sorry, Mom.'

'But you love him. And that's going to make everything all right.'

So much is missing here. So much of what might have been said.

Adrian struggled to free herself from Lennis's arms. To face her mother. Lennis had to let her go.

But even the wrong thing said is something said. A risk. A commitment to something. Lennis is an awfully good friend, but I wonder: why'd he say nothing? Why listen through all this?

'Mom,' Adrian said. Addressing only her mother. The various ways families shut each other out. 'I never wanted—'

Mary interrupted. 'So you're making me a grandmother. Do you know how old that makes me feel?'

For a second Adrian stared at her mother. Then flung herself away. Lennis reached for her again, but she ducked around him, her hair swinging against his face. She fled up the stairs sobbing. His face stung as if her hair had ripped it off the bones.

He couldn't face Mary. He spoke without looking at her. 'You didn't even touch her.'

'And you coddled her,' Mary replied bleakly. 'Nothing she does ever bothers you, does it?'

He walked away from her without another word.

When a family begins to resemble a church service, something's gone awry. Lennis didn't tell me all this until much later, but I could tell something was wrong. Too much politeness. "Yeah," I said when he finally began to talk about it. "I knew something was wrong. Couldn't say anything, but all those pleases and thank-yous whenever we worked together and I ate lunch with you. A few too many, I thought."

We were stacking straw. Lennis laughed and leaned against the stack. "We were that polite?"

"You were."

But they never talked about what needed talking about. I can't imagine what Adrian must have been going through. Poor girl. Right when she most needs her parents, they're not speaking—not to her or to each other. Except for please and thank you.

Lennis escaped into harvest. Soybeans were ready, a frost having dried them out, and he combined with a vengeance. A good excuse—as he himself said later—to stay away from the house. Just keep going. Watch the beans fall. Watch the tank fill up. Nothing like the momentum of a combine. Damn near a narcotic.

Then the old slough entered the picture. Through the dust rising off the circling reel one day, Lennis noticed a flash of white among the dried-out vines. As the combine sliced toward it, he made out the narrow neck and half-raised wings of a Canada goose. No one I know ever thrilled more to the sound of geese's honking coming down from the sky. In high school, once I was riding with him when he heard geese, and he stuck his head out the window looking for the flock and drove the car right into the road ditch. He hit a field approach and bounced back onto the road. I was screaming at him, seeing that approach looming, but he never heard me. Never saw. Kept his head in the wind, his eyes on the sky. Ended up mildly surprised at the rough ride. When we were back on the road, asked me what'd happened.

'Oh,' he said when I told him. Then: 'Awful big flock. Two hundred, I bet.'

So the sight of a Canada goose in his soybean field should have at least made him curious. But he was still numb from the rift Adrian's announcement had opened in the family. He kept his eyes on the sickle. He was almost on top of the bird before he realized it wasn't going to lift from the field. He jerked back on the hydrostatics, and the combine rocked to a halt, wailing as the threshing drum emptied. Lennis looked down from the dusty dials. The goose stretched its neck toward the flickering sickle. Its small, pointed tongue pulsed. Lennis waited for it to realize the enormity of the machine— the thirty-foot header, the cab looming like a cliff.

But the goose gave no ground.

Lennis had his hand on the hydrostatics. He felt nothing. If he pushed the lever, there would be a lurch, a small drop in RPMs. Then the field would lie flat before him again. On the return round he might find a few feathers. A red stain in the stubble. But most likely not. Most likely just dust.

But the wait. It was just enough, he told me, to take him

out of the harvest. To remember. How Adrian's hair had stung his face. "It's a funny thing," is the way he put it to me, "but as long as I was combining, I was able to forget it, pretty much. Adrian. Mary. Just go out and watch the beans fall. Watch the tank fill. But when that goose stopped me, I felt it all over again. Like it'd been waiting outside me for a chance to step back in. Where it really belonged. Her hair was like whips, Charlie. Whips, and then silence. And me and Mary with nothing good to say."

He disengaged everything, let the combine idle. Beyond the goose, an orange flag marked the tile intake. He was in the middle of the old slough. His father had refused to drain it. Lennis, more modern, seeing profit, had tiled it as soon as the old man died. No big deal. Everybody tiled. With taxes and all, it's hard to afford not to. Still, it's too bad. Geese and ducks used to descend like the sky itself in the fall. Bring the sky right down with them, like they were stitching it to the earth. Into all the sloughs this country contained. Everything turned wild in the fall. Lennis and I grew up in that—sloughs all over for exploring. And not just geese. Muskrats. Frogs. Herons. Egrets. Fox. Birds of all kinds. Most of that's gone now. When Lennis tiled his slough, that was about the last one around, and the geese just go on over now. High up. Sometimes we don't see them at all. And most of the other animals, too—replaced by emptiness. Crops, sure. But I look around sometimes and don't wonder why kids now prefer Nintendo. This land's more contained than the screen is.

On the other hand, Lennis let his slough come back,

and even I tell him he's crazy. And most people actually believe it.

He climbed down the ladder and trudged around the platform. The orange flag marking the tile intake snapped in the
breeze.

The bird half-raised its wings, threatening.

'Gwan,' Lennis said, waving his arms. 'Outta here!'

He stepped toward it.

The bird attacked.

Lennis jumped back, nearly tripping in the soybeans.
"You shoulda seen it, Charlie," he told me. "Came at me
faster'n I could believe. Wings back, hunched. Hissing.
Scared the crap out of me."

'Well, I'll be damned,' he muttered when he'd recovered
and the goose had retreated into the soybeans. He examined
the bird for signs of injury, but it had nothing of the listless,
droopy look of a sick animal. He went at it again, waving his
arms and yelling, but the goose just turned on him like it had
before, forcing him to retreat. He'd never seen anything
like it.

Dust hazed the sun. It mixed with the smell of diesel
exhaust and blew away. The wind dropped. Lennis, con-
founded by the goose, looked across the field. Saw his house.
Squatting on the land. Looking alone, isolated. Plunked
down. He thought of Mary and Adrian inside it. Saying nothing.

"The craziest thing," he told me, "but when the wind
stopped out there, it seemed that the stillness was all pouring
out of the house. Don't laugh now, Charlie. Stillness just
pouring out. And Adrian there. My daughter. I was combin-

ing soybeans, right? Had to be done. But I swear, Charlie, when I thought of her in that house like that, I wondered what the hell I was doing in the field."

⚜

Still, the goose was in the row. Even if he wanted to be with Adrian, he had to finish the round. No rule about it, but no farmer'd leave a round unfinished. He turned his attention back to the bird, windmilled his arms, yelled. The goose refused to move. Kept attacking. Lennis had to leap rows to avoid it. Sweat poured down his face, made furrows in the dust of his forearms.

And all for nothing. The bird looked healthy. There couldn't possibly be a nest here. It just plain refused to fly.

Damn animal.

He'd done enough. Tried. Taken the time to do the good thing. He couldn't wait here forever.

"I said screw it," he told me. "That's where I was at. Just screw the bird. Get on with things. If it thought it owned the field, all right."

He turned his back and climbed to the cab. The goose sank into the soybean vines. Lennis looked down at it. Then engaged the machinery. Belts squealed. The reel swept around. The judder and jar of the sickle came up through the metal. Lennis pulled down the throttle. The threshing drum moaned, rose to a pitch, howled. Soybean dust and dirt flew off the painted side of the combine and blew out the back. Obscured the lowering sun.

Lennis looked down once more.

The bird didn't move. Stupid. Stubborn.

All right. Lennis engaged the hydrostatics. The engine

bellowed, and the combine floated through the soybeans, devouring them.

The goose attacked. Ran right toward the sickle.

But Lennis saw, suddenly, why it wouldn't fly.

He jerked back on the hydrostatics so hard he lost his balance as the machine stopped. He slipped, knocked the lever forward again, the combine jerking, before he finally managed to stop it. Without even bothering to disengage the machinery, Lennis yanked the fuel cutoff. Everything fell to a strange, unnatural silence. When he slipped, Lennis lost sight of the bird. He had his eyes shut. The last thing he'd seen had been the bird and sickle, inches apart, rushing at each other.

He didn't want to look. "From above it, I saw the problem," he told me. "Its wings were catching on the vines. You know how stiff soybean vines get. Hell. It'd been trying to fly all the time. Raising its wings halfway, and me thinking it was threatening. All it was trying to do was get them over the vines so it could get out of there. Couldn't be done. Once it got into that row, it was trapped.

"I just put my head on the steering wheel with my eyes shut," he said. "Couldn't even look at what I'd done, Charlie."

And then—sound. He lifted his head. In wonder. There, standing inches from the header, its neck stretched to the sky, the goose was honking. Pouring out wildness. Muted through the glass, it sounded to Lennis as if it came from high clouds. Dropping down. A sound he hadn't heard in years. A sound he'd once driven into a road ditch trying to find.

He hadn't counted on the wild reflexes of the goose. When he slipped, it must have turned and fled the machine, its bluff called. Lennis listened to it, and his eyes filled. He told me that, and it's not an easy thing for a man to say.

"My love for the birds came back," he said. "Do you remember it, Charlie? How we loved them? We didn't just like them. We loved them. God, I'd forgotten. Just let myself forget. And not just the geese. Everything. Frogs, snakes, birds' nests, odd-shaped sticks. You remember, don't you?"

We were picking up rocks together when he told me this part of it. He wanted me to remember. I could tell. It was important to him. We leaned against the bale rack together, where we had a pile of rocks tumbled. I stared across his field. The slough he'd let come back was two hundred yards away. A mirror. A patch of sky. Framed by reeds. Set in the black earth.

"Yeah," I said. "I remember."

And I did. I remembered hiding in those reeds with him, just a couple of kids, watching the geese come down. Pour down. Like rain. Or snow. Drifting down to fill the slough. And us inside it all. Right there, with them. Inside the flock. Whispering.

Lennis nodded. Satisfied. "Yeah," he said. "Well, once I remembered that, I remembered how much I loved Adrian. Not just like I wanted her to be. But right now. As she was. And Mary, too. Like hunting, Charlie. How many times did we find something different than what were looking for?"

"That's a question," I said. "But hell. These rocks aren't picking themselves up."

So he started the combine again and backed it away from the goose. Shut the machine off, descended the ladder again. This time he could see the goose's wings catch in the brittle vines arching over the narrow rows, even hear the feathers scrape.

Lennis squatted down and regarded the bird for a while. Then stood. And ran.

Right at it.

The goose flared, hissing, its wings hunching again, its neck coming forward snakelike. But Lennis ran right into it. Scooped it up like a football. His feet caught in the vines as he grabbed the bird, and he stumbled. The goose's freed wings beat the air around Lennis, beat his head and ears. His face was caught in the vacuum and thrust of the wings, his ears full of their whistle and throw. One white confusion of hard air and bone, coming so fast he couldn't feel the blows. Pulling the goose away from him.

A good friend. It's all right to envy him this.

His whole purpose was to free the goose, but now that he held it, something in him resisted letting go. He hauled the bird in close and turned his head against its breast. His right ear pressed into the soft down. Then the tangle of soybeans clutched his feet. He fell. Throwing the goose up and away as he went down. But he'd heard for a moment an eternal thing. The goose's heartbeat, wild and brilliant, under the feathers. "The heart of the sky, Charlie," he said. "It was."

Then the ground rose up and jarred his wingless body. He hit and rolled and saw the bird tumble in the air. Straighten. Saw its wings cover the sky, come down together over him. He felt the backwash of air against his face. The goose lifted itself away from him as he lay on his back. It grew smaller. Smaller. The sky was a blue emptiness, with wind.

By the time he'd done chores, washed, and eaten, Mary was already in bed, reading. Avoiding talk. But he went in to her. He sat on the edge of the bed until she looked up from her book.

'How was your day?' he asked her.

'Fine.'

'I didn't get the beans finished.'

'Oh.'

'I ran into some trouble.'

She didn't respond. Went back to her book.

'How's Adrian?'

'She's fine.'

'That's nowhere near true, is it, Mary?' he said.

Her eyes swept the page.

'She's pregnant. Seventeen and pregnant, Mary. That's sure not fine. And we haven't even talked about it.'

Mary went completely still. "Completely still," he told me. "I reached out and touched her hair. And said, 'You know, Mary, some of this is turning gray.' "

"Just the kind of thing to endear a man to his wife," I said.

At which he smiled.

Mary's breath caught. Like a dry leaf swept against a wall by wind. She let her book drop into her lap.

'Hell, Mary,' he went on. 'You're old enough to be a grandmother. And you know what? That's not her fault.'

'Damn you,' she whispered.

'Sometimes we're all damn fools, Mary. I know you love

her. I do too. I love you, Mary. Go to her, will you? It's you she needs right now.'

Mary wept. Gripped his hand and wept.

They listened to their daughter moving in her room upstairs. Lennis looked out the window, a blank darkness beyond which the wind blew across the fields.

'That trouble I had,' he said. 'It was a Canada goose. It'd come down where that slough used to be. Like it knew it was supposed to be there. It couldn't get back up. Got between the rows and couldn't spread its wings.'

'What'd you do?'

'Tried to chase it up. It just attacked me.'

'So what'd you do?'

We were crouched in cattails when he got around to telling me this part of it. We'd heard high geese that morning, each of us on our separate farms, and I knew when my wife yelled at me that Lennis was on the phone what he'd be saying: "You must have chores done by now. Maybe we can see some set their wings."

"So what'd you tell her, then?" I asked.

"Pretty odd. For some reason, I didn't know what to say all of a sudden."

"Why not? Seems pretty clear to me."

"I don't know. Strange. Something in me just went private. And I couldn't tell her. I was afraid I'd lose it, maybe. Its heart. The sky's. That make any sense?"

"Probably not," I said.

"And Mary and I were as close right then as we'd maybe ever been."

"But you told me, Lennis."

"Yeah. Figure that out."

"So what'd you tell her?"

"I ran it through."

"You told her you ran it through the combine?"

He nodded. "In a way, I did, too. Would have. The bird just managed to escape first."

Mary was shocked.

'You ran it through the combine?' Her voice, he says, was thin as paper.

'It wouldn't move,' he said. 'I couldn't make it move.'

"You think that was the best thing to tell her?" I asked.

"I don't know. It's what I told her. In some ways it doesn't matter. I just wanted Adrian okay. And what the hell was that goose doing there anyway? You never see a single goose. It was like it was waiting for me. You able to explain that?"

"No. All I know is, you're losing a lot of money on this slough."

"Suppose I am."

"A lot of people think you're crazy. You know that?"

We heard a sound like dogs barking, far away in the sky. But in a moment our ears adjusted, and it wasn't barking at all. It was the clear bugle honk of geese.

"You can't afford to farm this way. You know that?"

But he was looking at the sky.

Wind Rower

1. The Neighbor

I was up on my silo attaching the blower pipes, and I happened to look across the field and saw Philip Hanson's wind rower, that new one with the hydrostatic drive, going around and around. Seemed crazy, but I figured that Pete was just having some fun the way kids do. I went on bolting on the pipes, but every once in a while I'd look up, and there'd be that wind rower, spinning in the middle of the field. After a while no way could I make sense of it. So when I finished getting the last pipe bolted into place, I climbed down and got in my pickup to go look.

I should have been more suspicious. I'd seen that thunderhead come out of the west. I was going to put on those blower pipes earlier, even, but decided to wait till that cloud passed. Didn't want to be up there during a storm. So I should have been thinking. Sometimes what's obvious is just too scary to think about, maybe. Or maybe because it's obvious, you don't think about it, your mind gets going too fast and starts to make things up, and then makes more things up, and you have all these explanations, and none are the right ones, but you're spending so much time seeing how they could be right that you ignore the real one.

So when I got over there and saw what was happening, I just sat on the road with the pickup idling and watched. Something was wrong, but I couldn't tell what, and you kind of hate to go driving across someone else's hay unless there's a clear and good reason. But the thing kept whipping around out there. I could hear the engine sound rising and falling. Then this feeling came to me, and I knew something was worse than just wrong. It was like when I was a kid I used to trap pocket gophers, take the legs to the extension agent for the bounty. I'd always carry a stick with me, and after I uncovered the trap, I'd slam the gopher on the head, put it out of its misery. Well, this one time, and I'd never done this before, I didn't uncover the trap, I just pulled up on the chain, figuring that if there was a gopher, it'd come up with the trap and I'd ding it on the head.

Well, I heard a funny sound as I was pulling. Like if a cat got its foot stuck in the mud and pulled it out. A small, sucking sound. And right away I felt kind of sick, like I'd just done something terrible, but I didn't know what, and there was nothing I could do about it, it was way too late. I stopped pulling and stood there with the chain in my hand, and I wanted to push the trap back into the ground the way it had been, and either walk away and not know anything, or else start all over. I even started to lower the chain, but of course it just folded, there was no way I could push the trap down even if it had made sense. Finally I just gave it a yank, pulled it clear up out of there, and jumped back away from it, you know how a person will do that.

The trap came up jangling, rusty and spewing dirt. And sure enough, it was sprung. But there wasn't no gopher in it. Just a leg, like a little clawed hand. All nasty and bleeding and torn. Fresh blood. From being pulled clear out of the socket. The gopher just hadn't come up. Too much weight of dirt pressing down. I stood there and held that chain, and watched blood gather and drop. Drop, drop, drop on the ground.

Sitting there in my pickup, that's how I felt again. That very way. Finally I just backed down the road till I came to Hanson's driveway, and I drove in and found Linda. I told her something bad had happened. I was that sure. Then I called the fire number.

2. The Fire Chief

Lord, I didn't hardly know how to respond to this one. People here don't make prank calls. Still, I thought it was some kind of joke at first. I've been chief only four months—the youngest one ever in Cloten. It's a volunteer force, but still, no twenty-eight-year-old has ever been chief. I trained and worked real hard for this job. I studied a lot. I know the procedures better than anyone. I've never been to college, but that's because I wanted to stay here. My wife and I are thinking of having kids, and this is a good place to raise kids. So that's why I'm here, still. By choice, not because I'm less than smart, or a screw-up.

But I figured right away that someone was testing me. I figured even it could be someone else on the force, trying to see how the kid was handling the job. "A wind rower out of control," I said. "What's it doing? Chewing through fences?"

I probably shouldn't have said that last thing. But the guy came back: "No. It's spinning circles. At full throttle."

"Is there somebody on it?" I asked. Right away I thought that was a dumb question, but there was a pause, like the caller was debating how to answer, and I figured I had him, this was a prank.

But then, real quiet, murmured, like he wanted only me to hear and there was someone maybe close by, he said: "Something's happened. I don't know what. Maybe he's unconscious. But someone's got to stop that thing."

That's when my heart started pumping. From the way he was uncertain. To tell the truth, I couldn't imagine what he was talking about. I knew what a wind rower was, but I was never a farmer, lived in town all my life, and I couldn't quite see the problem. He said it was out of control—spinning circles and out of control—but that didn't really sink in. How could it?

Procedure says, assume the worst. If you're going to respond to a call, go with everything you got. But this wasn't a fire. It was more than a kitten in a tree, that old story, but I didn't know how much more. The machine wasn't going anywhere. It didn't seem like a major emergency to me. I'm not saying I wasn't concerned about whoever was on it. I was concerned, real concerned. But I figured I could probably handle it alone.

Maybe I screwed up. And if I did, I'm saying it was my fault. That's part of the job of being chief. But given the information I had, I couldn't see getting fifteen men away from their jobs and roaring out to the Hanson farm with trucks and nothing to do with them. Besides that, the Town Council is always telling me to keep costs down. And people've told me I did good, that in my position they would've done the same thing. A lot of people've said that to me.

Anyway, I figured I'd go alone. I could always radio back for help. Close to the Hanson place, I passed a line of pea combines from the canning factory, going from one field to another, and when I got around them, I could see the trouble. Just like the caller'd said, the machine was out in the middle of Hanson's hay field, spinning away, with three people watching it, two of them real close—Philip and Linda Hanson—and the other, their neighbor, Tom Jerrold, kind of away. I pulled off the road and down into the ditch and bounced across the hay, over the windrows.

I drove right up to Jerrold and got out, not too fast, not wanting to seem panicky. The machine was just howling and whining. "Fill me in," I yelled, standing next to Jerrold and studying the thing whipping around. He looked at me like I was nuts or something, and I got real uncomfortable. It's like that a lot, being younger. People don't believe you know what you're doing. I just looked back at him.

"You got trucks coming?" he yelled.

"No," I yelled back. "There's no fire, is there?"

"Jesus Christ!" He spit, and it gobbed up on an alfalfa plant, one that hadn't been cut, and rolled down the stem. Disgusting, I thought. Then he shouted: "How you plan to stop that thing?"

"I got to take a look at the situation first," I yelled.

Then all of a sudden Jerrold grabs me by my shirt and comes in real close to me, his face all unshaven and smelling of sweat and silage. I was for sure going to be smacked, I thought, and I was getting ready to fight back. I'd had some martial arts classes over in Clear River—just about took the test for my brown belt, in fact—and I know how to take care of myself. But I got to admit, Lord! he was strong. Big old fists like anvils on my shirt. I mean, I'm jerking away, jerking hard, and I'm not moving at all. He just keeps drawing me in, like I'm at the end of a tow cable and he's the winch.

Then all of a sudden I realize he's not angry at all, he's got something entirely else on his mind. He's looking past me, over my shoulder. Then, right in my ear, real quiet, down under the scream of the machine, he says: "Get an ambulance out here. That boy's in tough shape up there. He might even be dead."

He stops but keeps right on holding me, and I get real uncomfortable. But he has me tightened and screwed down with those arms of his, unless I want to rip my shirt pulling away. Then, no louder than before, he says: "That's the boy's mother over there. And father. It took the both of us to keep her from running right into that thing. She was on her way when I tackled her."

Then he lets me go. I look up at the machine, howling around in a haze of dust and smoke, grinding, groaning, pounding into the ground, and I imagine Linda running right toward it, all desperate and her hair streaming out behind her, and Philip too dazed to even know what she's doing, and then Jerrold comes from behind her and tackles her, hard, just rams her down into the ground, and her breath grunts out of her, *whoof,* but there's no sound because the machine is so loud it's like everything is silent, and I see her head kind of bend back, then whipslam into the stubble, and she's twisting to hit Jerrold, and he's got those arms of his like steel cables wrapping her, but even then she's getting away, slippery and tough as a cat, and then Philip comes over real slow and dazed yet and grabs her and sits on her, and he's stronger than Jerrold even, not wiry, just solid as a rock, and finally she just quits moving, and all the while, above them, the wind rower is whip, whip, whipping around, the sound of it rising and falling as it swings.

It gives me a real funny feeling to picture all this, but I don't let on. I straighten out the front of my shirt, then reach through the window of the pickup and call for an ambulance. But I still can't see what good a fire truck is going to do, I just can't see it, so I don't ask for one, leastways not until I can survey the situation a little more thoroughly.

I put down the radio and turn back to the problem. Linda is watching me, expecting me to do something, and she's crying, not doing anything about it, not even trying to wipe the tears away. Philip is watching the wind rower, and holding her so tight she's just pressed against his chest, but he's so still it don't seem natural, like he's frozen or turned to wood.

I decide they're far enough away from the machine. You're always supposed to move people back away from things, to allow for safety and freedom of movement, non-interference. I got to admit it was some relief I didn't have to go over and ask them to move back some.

I study the wind rower. Thinking of Linda Hanson running into it'd given me the creeps, but the more I study the situation, the more I see how it'd be possible to get the thing stopped. It's really ripping around, but I start to feel this rhythm, and I can see how you could wait for the engine to go by and then sprint for the center. You couldn't just go charging in there like Linda'd tried, but if you timed it right, it could be done. And once you're in the center, you could even walk, take your time, and climb the ladder and pull back the stick and shut the thing off and bring the boy down. The more I look at it, the more it seems possible, and I wonder why Jerrold or Hanson haven't already done it.

But then I go closer, and Lord! a real strange feeling comes over me. I got plenty of guts. I was a football star in high school, not because I was big, but because I'd go after anybody. I'd come out of games all bruised and bleeding, but I didn't care. And some guys, for instance, when they climb that big ladder truck and hang ninety feet in the air, they can't take it, they turn white, and once a guy even puked. But none of that ever bothered me.

But this . . . I mean, this'd give granite the shivers. For one thing, from closer up I can see the boy better, and I got to agree with Jerrold. He looks dead. He's a tall kid, he played basketball, and he's slumped over the machine's control stick, and he's absolutely not moving up there. He's turning, of course. His face comes around every few seconds, all white and blank-looking, and almost upside down he's bent so far over. And his clothes are all scorched and I can see this black skin, burned and bubbly, along his right shoulder. But the worst is his hair. Curled up like charred fur on his scalp.

I got to admit I hadn't never actually seen a dead person before. I mean, out of a casket. I've been on enough fire calls, but they're always barns or grass fires or haystacks, or not even that, like when those Crandall kids set that abandoned barn on fire, that was the very first fire I helped fight when I was a new volunteer, but what'd we even bother to go out there to fight that fire for, that barn was just going to fall apart anyway? I don't know how to say this without sounding, what? Sadistic? 'Cause it's just the opposite, really. But every time a call comes in, I kind of hope it'll be someone trapped in a building. I mean, I don't hope it. Of course I don't hope it. I'd just like to save someone some time. I got all this training and for what? I'd really like it, to be the one to save somebody. But there's never the chance.

Sometimes when we're pumping water full blast on another haystack, I wonder why we don't just let it burn. The water's ruining it bad as the fire. But we all pretend there's nothing more important in the world than getting that fire out. And afterward people will tell us what good work we did. But I'll go home sometimes and just feel kind of empty. Like . . . is this all there is to it? Is this all there's ever going to be?

But right in front of me now is someone to be saved. I mean, I got to assume he's alive. The trouble is, I don't really believe it—not the way that white face, upside down, goes past me every few seconds, eyes just swinging over me like a searchlight at an airport would. And the other trouble is . . . well, like I said, it'd be possible to wait for the engine to swing by and then sprint for the center. But you got to picture this.

This whole machine is running, see, full blast. The reel is turning, the spring-teeth on it like claws coming up and over, then ripping back down toward the sickle, and the sickle is chattering away, those triangular blades a blur when the platform swings by, snicking back and forth, all green-stained and shiny, nasty-looking. I've heard of cats being cut in half by those sickles. The boy's weight is pushing the stick as far ahead as it'll go and all the way to the right, so the right drive wheel is spinning backwards as fast as it'll go, and the left one forwards just as fast. The hydrostatics are just groaning keeping those wheels going. This thing is spinning around so fast you can hardly keep up with it. They'll do, I've heard, over twenty miles an hour straight ahead.

And the engine hanging over that big caster wheel—it's just whipping around. It's bouncing in the air and slamming back down on the ground. I can feel it in my feet, right through the soles of my boots. Thudding and sickening. Real heavy. It's like if you cast a capital letter T in iron, about fourteen feet long and four high, two tons' worth, and put lugged wheels on the ends of the crossbar and a wicked sickle and a big old reel chattering and sweeping around inside the crossbar, and then set those lugged wheels going in opposite directions, fast. And the vertical bar has the engine, see, hanging over a caster wheel, and blasting out gasoline fumes and noise—if you can kind of picture that whipping around in its own haze, in a track it's already cut into the stubble, you got some idea of what this thing was like.

Still, I can see a line—like running a football, how you can sometimes see your way through the tacklers, and you know you have the down even though it's eight yards yet and there's defense all around. I can see how I could make it to the center, and like I said, once you're there, it's slow. The boy up on the platform, he's coming around every couple seconds, but not fast. Kind of dreamlike and peaceful, unconcerned-like. If you could just get past the outside circles safe.

And I even prepare myself. I stand real close, so close that the heat of the exhaust blasts me every time it goes by. I look in there and visualize the line I'd have to follow. I get all tensed, and I tell myself, five more swings and I go. And then

I count them down. Five. Four. Three. Two. One.

But my legs don't move. They're all tensed and ready, but they don't move. So I try again, a different number, seven this time, and count it down. But the more I count, the bigger that platform gets, and every time it goes by, I see those sickle blades shimmering back and forth, all blurry and sharp. And I got boots on, and they're not made for running, they feel awful heavy. So I'm all tensed and ready again, but I get down to one and I don't go, I just stand there like my whole body has a charley-horse cramp.

So I try ten this time, but about halfway down the count I quit seeing the line entirely, or myself following it. Instead I see myself tripping and stumbling, or I see my boots moving real slow, like one of those slow-motion wildlife films, and I just can't speed them up. And I see the back of the platform coming around, and I'm nowhere near the center yet, and then, Lord! I'm looking over my shoulder, and the whole gaping maw of the thing is right behind me, or I've stumbled and I'm laying in the hay, and the platform is growing like the whole world on me. And when I'm down around number three, I get to where I imagine those pointed sickle guards poking right into my ribs and the sickle slicing away at me, cutting right into my bones. And at two, I see it cutting me off at the ankles, and me falling backwards, grabbed by the reel, and run through the auger and out through the hole in the back, and then mashed right into the ground and stubble by the drive wheels. And my feet sitting there by themselves.

And I don't even say the one. I just go all untensed and let the engine go by. I look up, and the boy's face is moving past me again, just moving on by, not caring what I do or don't do. I let it swing by, and turn and walk away.

Linda is watching me. I catch her eye but I don't hold it. I look at Philip, but it's like his eyes have turned to stones, not seeing anything. Then Linda starts to go down to her knees, like they're melting and she's sinking right into the ground. She sinks that way, real slow, then all of a sudden drops. She's holding her eyes on the machine, on her knees in the stubble, and her hands are kind of fluttering in front of her, like they're picking flowers, but there're no flowers there. I can hardly stand to watch her, but I can't not watch either.

She sinks even further, she bends at the waist and just kind of wilts, and her face goes into the stubble, with her hair falling around it. She sinks until she's curled up the way a baby sleeps, only her body is shaking, rising and falling. Philip is standing with one hand reached out to her. Then he sinks, too, with his hand still reached out, coming closer and closer to her. Finally he's kneeling beside her, and his hand is on her back, moving in little circles there, but everything else about Philip is still. His face is like a blank, dark window just before a brick hits it. And that one hand going around in little circles on her back.

I feel like a jerk. I feel like I'm the one just certified it: too bad, he's dead. I go up to Jerrold. I feel like crying. But I don't let on. I get real close, so I don't have to yell. "We'll just have to let it run out of gas," I say. If he wanted to hit me, I wouldn't care. Then I feel his arm around my shoulders, tight as a vise. It's kind of comforting, really.

And really, I kind of forget what happened after that. It took an hour and a half for the thing to run out of gas. The ambulance came, and someone managed to get Linda and Philip in there and laying down. Other people showed up,

Linda's sister for one, who I was awful relieved to see. And we all just stood around and waited.

A lot later I thought I could have called a boom truck out and had myself lifted over to the boy. Or I could have run my pickup right into the thing and stopped it that way, smashed things up quite a bit, of course. And maybe, even, I could have made it in there running. But he had to be dead, didn't he? Right away, soon as that bolt hit him. He had to be. I mean, he never moved a bit the whole while.

Jerrold's the only one who saved a life. And I don't think he knows it. That's what's so crazy. And she didn't even want to be saved.

3. THE MOTHER

I try to make sense of this. But there's no sense to be made. I stand in my kitchen. I have sheer curtains on the windows. In the breeze they move like veils of water white and falling, white and falling. We took a trip to the mountains once. We found a little waterfall. It came from a crack in the ground and fell a long, long ways. There were people all around, gathered on the road. We stopped anyway. They were all snapping pictures. Philip got out the camera and started to snap pictures too. Peter was eight, and I kept my hand on his shoulder. The road was curving and busy, and I was afraid he would go running across to look at the water more closely.

But he just stood there. He let my hand rest on his shoulder. I wanted to put it around him and hug him and stand close like that, watching. But he was at that age when that would have embarrassed him, and I was afraid that he would shake me off entirely. So I let my hand just rest on his shoulder. It must have seemed natural to him. He didn't know I was restraining myself. How my heart was wrenched. He was wondering at the falls. And I missed them because I wanted so much to share them completely with him.

I wanted so much. And I missed them. But they must have been falling dreamily. They must have been all spumy and white. Because he stood there for the longest time and then asked: "Are they falling up or falling down?" And maybe I saw how the water flaked in the wind. Maybe I saw how it had turned to a sheet that maybe was moving and maybe was not. But I answered: "Down, of course. Things always fall down."

"Even water?"

"Even water."

Again I wanted to hug him. I wanted to kneel beside him and hug him right there. All I was aware of was how much I was holding back. So that I could keep this least touch of my hand on his shoulder.

Cameras were clicking all over. They were like bugs in the breeze, loud, clacking bugs.

"Do you think if you had a rowboat and rowed real hard, you could row to the top?" he asked me.

And maybe I saw how the water seemed solid, as bright as marble and as sure. Maybe I saw how it looked like you could drive an oar or a pole right into it, get a good grip, and push. But I answered: "No. There's nothing there, really."

And I almost gripped his shoulder, almost tightened my hold. I felt my muscles begin it. But I stopped them and just imagined them doing it. I imagined the tips of my fingers pressing deep until they felt his marvelous bones. I just imagined it, and he never moved. He stayed with the falls.

"Not even if the wind blew you up?"

"No. Not even then."

Then Philip came back, and he said: "Beautiful, isn't it? We got some great pictures. What do you think, Pete?"

And still he didn't move. He just kept looking at the falls, and he said: "I feel the water on my face. Do you feel the water on your face?"

And maybe I felt how the wind was softly laden with it, how the wind was cool and wet, filled with the spray that maybe was rising and maybe was falling. But I answered: "We better go now. We have a long way to go yet today."

He goes around and around. In my mind yet, around and around. I see his white face, as cold and solid as marble, come around and around and around.

I remember my hand on his shoulder. How I went no further because I wanted to so badly. I was afraid he would shake me off.

So what if he had? There would have been a moment, a single moment, before he knew what was happening, before he could break away. And in that moment I would have known the spume and the spray and my boy. I would have felt the world on my face.

Making the News

E D finished Dog Killing Chickens yesterday. It moans in the wind, like it's pulling the sound of the earth out, so deep and low you almost don't hear it, more feel it and get tense below your ribs. When Gary was a kid, he knocked the cover off a baseball, and I found it, the string coiled so tight it wasn't string, hard enough to hurt. I woke and my nerves were like that below my ribs. I massaged the coiling out and got breathing again before I actually noticed the sound below the bed and house, like it was coming up from the well, a wolf running through the aquifer, howling far away.

"My land," I whispered. "What noise is that?"

I didn't know Ed was awake until he spoke. "The new one," he said.

"It makes a sound like that?"

"Seems to."

"You planned it?"

"Maybe."

"Aren't there enough windsounds out here all the time, Ed, without you inventing a new one?"

"No inventin', Charlene. Just findin' what's there."

We were both on our backs, staring at the ceiling. The wind ran past the dark window, and the sound rose and fell, low and earthy.

"Can you stop it?" I asked.

"Not unless the wind stops."

"Wind never stops. It'll drive them newsmen crazy tomorrow."

"More likely drive'm sane."

The sound was making pictures in my head now. I could see a wolf running, cloudlegs reaching, mistfur curling back, running through the earth.

"You gonna let'm follow you around, Ed? Let'm take pictures of you welding? Pictures of the cars?"

"That's just what I need, ain't it? Some newstwerp in the shop with a camera in my face."

"Why you letting them come, then?"

"Pride, Charlene. The oldest sin."

I knew better. "Should get yourself on *Oprah*," I said. "Must be a show about people making statues in their backyards."

"And dressing in drag. And I don't make statues."

"I know. Sorry."

"Big difference between statues and sculptures."

"I know. Ed, I gotta sleep. What are you going to do about it?"

"Nothin' I can do. Like I said."

"I ain't asking can you stop the noise. I'm asking how you gonna help me sleep."

"Got no idea, Charlene."

"No? Moan louder'n it, Ed. In my ear. We ain't too old for that yet."

I reached over and stuck my hand inside his pajamas. He waited a while, not saying anything, not moving. After some time, he said:

" 'Pears we ain't, Charlene."

"Appears not," I said.

He laid his hands upon me then. I should've known when he first did that in the backseat of his Packard, how many years ago? that he was going to be some kind of artist. I've never been tired of Ed's hands since.

When I woke up, Ed was already in the shop, working on Don't Fall In Love In the Woods It'll Only Make You Miserable. "Ed," I'd said when I first heard that title, "that sounds like a country-western song."

"Don't worry," he'd replied. "The plaque'll read just 'Love In the Woods.' "

Dog Killing Chickens was still moaning, and I shut my eyes. I imagined the mistwolf again, sweeping through the pores of rock, until I spooked myself and opened my eyes and saw my coffee shaking.

Who would've thought?—a Minneapolis TV station coming down here. It was Hell's Angel Contained that got them interested. I told Ed, you put that thing at the end of the driveway, you're going to attract attention. At first it was just local people. They'd stop on the road and sit in their cars and look.

"You see'm, Charlene?" Ed'd say. "Wondering what the hell that's supposed to be. Don't even know they know. That's what really gets 'em."

At first I didn't like Hell's Angel Contained. It changed the whole view. Or me looking at the view. Used to be I'd look up the driveway and see nothing but corn or soybeans, or stubble in the winter. But now, off that sculpture, my eye seems to bounce back to me, like I'm seeing myself seeing. The thing comes out of the ground in two big curving wings, the roofs and hoods of the '52 Fairlane and the '61 Bonneville. The wings come up like they're growing, and there's a little hunched-over figure inside them. And above them—welded to their tips so it looks like it's floating in the air—is a big cogwheel, and inside it are all these little gears from the engines of the cars, gears and pulleys, circles inside circles. It all looks like it's floating, but also like it's going to fall down and flatten the hunched-over figure inside.

Pretty soon cars we didn't know started stopping up there, and then there was an article in the *Clear River Gazette*. The reporter discovered the other sculptures around the place, and took pictures. After that we had a steady stream of traffic on the road, and people coming into the place to look around. Then the guy from Channel 13 in Minneapolis called.

I set my coffee in the sink and went outside. They'd be here at ten. Man Flying, Ed's first sculpture, was shining in the sun. You can't see the supports that hold it to the galvanized roof of the silo, so it looks like it's hanging up there. It's a rectangular cube with a couple more steel cubes running off it at angles, like a T with the horizontal bar tipped up. Or

like a man flying, or diving, a swan dive. The whole thing
tips like gravity's just starting to pull it down. Ed had me
worried sick when he was attaching it, crawling around seventy feet up on the roof of the silo, bolting.

I yelled at him: "I'll leave you if you don't come down."

"No you won't," he called back, calm as a cow.

"Don't be so sure."

"All I got's you and the welding. You wouldn't leave."
He drilled another hole, the sound like metallic thunder echoing in the silo. When he pushed against the drill, I was sure
he'd slip off. "Course you and the welding, Charlene, that's
quite a bit," he said when he'd drilled the hole. "You alone's
quite a bit."

"Old men should learn their limits," I said.

I looked up at Man Flying now, the chrome strips on the
leading edges of the arms, or wings, blinding in the sun. Then
I went around the corner of the shop and walked through
Thunderstruck Boy. It was a big metal horizontal T-shaped
platform inside a circle of small upright t's that Ed says are
people. On top of the big T is another figure like the ones
on the ground around it. Coming out of this figure's head is
a jagged, zigzag piece of metal, ragged from the cutting torch.
It goes up thin and bright, then branches, and Ed's got it
attached to the roof of the shop with thin rods he painted
blue so you can hardly see them against the sky—it looks like
those jagged streaks come out of the figure's head and shoot
into the sky with nothing holding them.

I walked through the sculptures and opened the door to the
shop. The spit and hum of welding hit me, and the smell of
burning flux. I stepped around the bolt bins and watched the
flame, bright blue, with smoke curling away from it, throwing

shadows up and down the walls. Ed was laying a bead. I stared straight into the flame, bright beyond fire, like a small blue sun. Ed held it even and controlled at the end of the rod, floating over the metal. Sometimes when I watch it, it seems to burn the past and future away, or fuse them, filling my eyes.

Ed pulled the wand up and away. The flame crackled, a hollow gasping sound came out of it, the welder moaned, and the light ended. Ed flipped back the helmet before I could duck around the bolt bins.

"Charlene," he said, "you're going to burn your eyes out."

"You've told me," I said.

"It's ultraviolet light."

"It going okay?"

"Listen to me. Why you think I wear this thing?" He smacked the helmet.

I didn't say anything. Some fascinations are too private for explanation—or love. Ed reached over and snapped the welder off.

"Love In the Woods," I said.

He nodded. "Got the Packard into this one."

"The Packard? Ed! The Packard?"

"Good thick steel," he said.

"But Ed, the Packard?"

"Don't make 'em like they used to," he said. "Try making Love In the Woods with a Toyota. Wouldn't stand up."

"But Ed," I said. "Don't you remember the Packard?"

"Course I do," he said. "Toyota wouldn't'na stood up to any a those times either. Course the Packard finally wore out, too."

I walked over and touched the metal. The blue paint was scorched near the weld. The steel was as warm as if it were alive. "So many memories," I said.

"Been sitting in the grove for forty years," he said. "Love in the woods, see? But only you and me'll ever know."

Right at ten the white newsvan turned into the driveway. I picked the ducks out of the cattle tank and set them on the ground. Ed'd offered a few years ago to bury the tank at ground level, since we had no cattle anymore, and the ducks could have their own easy-access pond. But Gary'd started putting the ducks into the tank when he was a kid, and when he left, I'd continued; it'd just be another absence if I stopped.

By the time I'd set all the ducks on the ground, I could read the big letters on the side of the van: NEWSFIRST ON 13. As if any of those guys get to news first. I held the last duck close, remembering how Gary had loved the oilclean smell, then set it down. Ducks always look like they know where they're going. They probably don't, except that where they get is always where they were going. I watched them set off, then walked around the empty grain bins. The van'd stopped near the house, but no one had gotten out. I could see the passenger was Paul Alcorn.

He saw me coming and opened his door. The wind didn't move his hair, but his smile looked real. "You must be Charlene Olsen," he said, holding out his hand.

I gave him mine. "And you're Paul Alcorn. No must-be needed there."

He laughed. "That's the trouble with my job," he said. "No hiding."

I surprised myself by deciding I might like him. The driver got out, and then another guy stooped out of the back—Oliver Ringburton, the Channel 13 artscaster. That's what they call him, like in sportscaster. He tended to stick to plays and galleries in Minneapolis or St. Paul. He was wearing his tweed, and his hair hung down around his head like curtains. He brushed his coat off and peered through his little glasses. "So, is this the place?" he asked Paul Alcorn, without looking at me.

"You think so?" Paul Alcorn asked.

Oliver Ringburton was looking over my shoulder at Semi Accident (With Cattle). The thing took up the entire space between the granary and the south end of the grove.

Oliver Ringburton sniffed, then walked past us to the sculpture.

"Had to bring him," Paul Alcorn said quietly.

"You two must've had a good trip out here," I said.

He laughed so loudly Oliver Ringburton turned and glared.

"Arnie, bring that camera," he commanded. The other man stuck a camera on his shoulder and stepped quietly around us.

Linda Hansen's car turned in the driveway. She must've seen the van. She was the only one Ed'd ever asked could he do a sculpture. We were friends with her and Philip, and it'd been real hard on them when Pete'd got hit by lightning. Then Philip'd died five years later, went through ice on a snowmobile on Judgement Lake. One evening after that, Ed got up after supper and said he was going out. He came back after dark, quieter than usual, so I asked: "Where you been, Ed?"

"Linda Hansen's."

"What were you doing there?" He had me pretty curious.

"What you suppose? She a lonely widow and all?"

"And you Clark Gable," I said.

"I'm dedicatin' a sculpture, but thought I should ask her."

"Pete?"

He nodded.

"She say okay?" He nodded again. "Broke down and bawled. Wasn't expectin' that."

"No? Ed, sometimes I swear you're the dumbest smart man I ever met."

Linda pulled up and parked beside the newsvan. I introduced her to Paul Alcorn. Arnie came back. "Paul," he said, "how do you want to do this?"

Oliver Ringburton was walking around Accident making notes. Paul looked like he might call him over, then decided against it. "Let's talk to the artist first," he said.

"He's welding right now," I said. "Might not take to the interruption."

"Footage of him welding'd be good," Paul said.

I nodded to the shop. "In there, then."

We all came around the bolt bins and watched Ed lay a bead. The light danced down the metal, scattering blue, jerky shadows. Ed was making a forest out of the Packard, turning tie rods and bolts, even the crankshaft, into winter trees, barren and branching. He'd cut a river channel out of the curving hood with a cutting torch. We stood there watching the arc until he finished the bead and pulled the wand away. He flipped the small, dark-glass part of the helmet up and peered at us through the rectangle of clear plastic inside.

"Gonna burn your eyes out," he said.

His voice wasn't too clear from inside the helmet. Paul Alcorn looked at me. "Shouldn't watch an arc," I said.

Paul Alcorn blinked and looked into the darkest corner of the shop, trying to compensate. "Mr. Olsen," he said. "I'm Paul Alcorn from Channel Thirteen. Could we talk to you?"

Ed reached over and hit the switch on the welder. It clunked off, and the shop went silent. I heard the mistwolf howling. Ed hung the wand on the edge of his welding table and sat down on the hood of the Packard.

"This is for television, Mr. Olsen," Paul Alcorn said. "The helmet? Could you take it off?"

"Could," Ed replied.

Paul Alcorn just looked at him.

"You come for the sculptures, right?" Ed asked. "Not some human-interest story?"

"Well," Paul Alcorn said, "I'm not sure we made the distinction."

The shop door opened and closed. Paul Alcorn glanced around. He'd finally heard the sound out of Dog Killing Chickens but didn't quite know it yet. Oliver Ringburton came around the bolt bins. "Say," he said, looking down at his notepad and just about running into Linda. "I need to talk . . ."

His voice trailed off at the sight of Ed.

"Mr. Ringburton, the artscaster," Ed said.

"I prefer art critic," Oliver Ringburton said, glancing at Paul Alcorn. "Are you . . ."

"Ed Olsen," Ed finished for him.

"Well, Mr. Olsen, I'd like to talk to you."

"Be glad to."

Oliver stared for a moment at Ed, then looked nervously at the rest of us. Even I found it disconcerting to have Ed talking out from under that helmet. Made him seem half machine.

"I guess the helmet stays on," Paul Alcorn said to Oliver.

"Oh. Well, then. Mr. Olsen, could we maybe start with where you got your training?"

"Cloten," Ed replied.

"Cloten?"

"Learned to weld in Marvin Klinkleberg's welding shop. Part-time when I was young."

"I don't mean that. I mean the designing."

Ed didn't answer right away. Dog Killing Chickens pitched and lowered. Paul Alcorn looked at me, puzzled, and Oliver stood with his pen ready.

"How's the designing different than the doing?" Ed asked.

"But surely you studied art."

"Glad you think so. Most probably I did. But suppose me and, say, Henry Moore had coffee down at the Cloten Chat 'N' Chew every day and he gave me all sortsa pointers. Would that make those sculptures out there better, you think, than if Marvin Klinkleberg taught me to weld, and the rest was just me and the metal?"

Oliver Ringburton didn't seem to have an opinion. Arnie turned the camera on him, swinging it quietly to whoever interested him. I decided to be careful about opening my mouth. Arnie was too easy to forget about. With Paul Alcorn there, and Oliver Ringburton, you tended to think about them, since they had the faces. But Arnie was the real show here, just disappearing and getting everything all smooth and quiet.

"Well, Mr. Olsen," Oliver Ringburton finally said, "that's an interesting question."

"Point is," Ed said, "you're trying to turn this into a story about me insteada the sculptures."

"Maybe," I suggested, "we should all go out and look at them together."

I caught Ed's eye, saw him wink through the glass. "Good idea," he said, and got up and led us through the door.

The ducks were waddling up from the empty grain bins. Arnie swung the camera over them, the only thing moving on the farm, then focused on Hell's Angel Contained for a while.

"What's that noise?" Paul Alcorn asked.

"Dog Killing Chickens," Ed replied.

"What?"

"Dog Killing Chickens," I said. "A sculpture. The wind does that."

"What noise?"

No one answered Oliver Ringburton. If you couldn't hear it, what could anyone say?

We were standing in Thunderstruck Boy. Oliver Ringburton looked down at his notepad. "You use a lot of Christian imagery," he said. "Would you comment on that?"

"Hadn't noticed," Ed said.

Sometimes the man embarrasses me, even after all these years. Even for Ed, he was being pretty ornery. But Oliver Ringburton just went on. "Well, take this sculpture here," he said, pleased to be able to explain things. "A large cross with other cross figures surrounding it, an abstract crucifixion scene. And the 'boy' is Christ, the son. But why is the large cross horizontal? And does the lightning symbolize a storm, or his spirit leaving his body? Or both?"

He really was pleased with himself. Ed considered what he'd said.

"Sure," he finally said. "Why not?"

Behind me, Linda Hansen drew in her breath.

"Of course," Ed went on, "it could be a windrower."

"It sure is," Linda whispered.

"A what?" Oliver asked.

"Windrower. Swatter."

"Swather," I said.

"Swather?"

"What's wrong with that man?" Linda whispered.

"Of course!" Paul Alcorn exclaimed suddenly. "I see. And the boy is running it."

"Exactly," Linda said out loud. Everyone looked at her, including Arnie's camera.

"Well, that's right," she said.

"What's a swather?" Oliver asked.

"A machine," Ed replied, behind the mask. "Cuts hay and grain. Looks like a big T on wheels. Or a cross if you want."

"That's what this is about?"

"Have to be about something?"

"What about this one?" Paul Alcorn asked.

We strolled to Semi Accident (With Cattle). The ducks were chasing bugs around it. It was Ed's biggest piece, two big rectangular cubes of car steel in front of a brick wall he'd built. The larger cube was balanced so it stood on edge, and the shorter one, which stuck halfway through the wall, stood on its corner. Ed'd cut slits into the long cube with the cutting torch, and through the slits you could see figures made of gears and tie rods and pistons, tangled together but separate, too. Looking through the slits, you'd just think you saw an individual figure and then you'd notice it was tangled with another. When the sun cast shadows, it doubled the confusion. Ed'd welded the cube shut so you couldn't get inside to sort any of it out.

"How'd you get it to balance like that?" Paul asked.

"Long posts going into the ground to anchor it," Ed said.

"It looks like it's floating on edge."

"Look inside," Ed invited.

Paul and Oliver stepped to the cube. The closer you get to it, the more it looks like it's going to fall on you. The ducks chased bugs right under it, but Paul and Oliver got slower and slower as they approached. Finally they peered through the slits, and looked for a long time while Arnie held the camera on them.

"That drives me nuts," Paul said when they finally turned away.

"Intriguing," Oliver Ringburton said.

"Is this one 'about' something?" Paul asked.

"Could be," Ed said.

Everybody in Cloten knows about the time Two-Speed Crandall wrecked his semi and killed himself, and Leo Gruber had to spend all day getting his dead and dying cattle off the truck. I caught Ed's eye again and saw him shrug.

"I must admit," Oliver Ringburton said, "there's more to your work than I expected. Have you ever considered smaller pieces?"

"White-cube stuff," Ed said. "Wouldn't touch it."

"White-cube stuff? You've read—?"

"Wouldn't put stuff in a gallery," Ed said. "This stuff belongs where I put it. You got to have context. Otherwise you got a statue, not a sculpture. Liquid art. Won't set you down and put you in a place. But that there will."

"Well," Oliver Ringburton said.

"Try pickin' that up and puttin't in a gallery," Ed went on. "Give you a hernia, but not much else. Now, I'm getting back to work. You look around."

He turned and walked back toward the shop. "Well," Paul said, "I guess, Arnie, you go with Oliver and get footage of the sculptures. Charlene, could you tell us what's here?"

Linda had stayed back at Thunderstruck Boy, and it was only the four of us. "Just stay on the building site," I said, "and you'll find them all. There's the ones you've seen: Thunderstruck Boy and this one, and Man Flying on the silo, and Dog Killing Chickens, that's the newest one, in the pasture, and Hell's Angel Contained, you passed that when you came in. Then there's Mammoths Resurrected by the rock pile behind the cattle yards, and Cure Of the Goose a bit beyond it, and then Sacrificial Hawk, Old Man Killing Goats, and Mother's Abdication."

Arnie and Oliver took off and left me and Paul Alcorn alone. He looked up the driveway at Hell's Angel Contained, that big wheel floating over those wings.

"Satan?" he asked, nodding.

"Hell's Angel," I said. "Why not?"

He's no dummy. "You sound like Ed," he said.

"We've been married long enough."

"Why'd he start all this?"

"You think these pieces are good?"

"I do."

"And Oliver?"

"Oliver. All the way out here he complained about having to leave Minneapolis just to see someone's big Erector Set. But the stuff's got to him."

"That's why Ed started," I said. "Because he's good."

"Yes," he said. "But it's more than that."

Sometimes insight, especially unexpected, if it doesn't scare you, can set up vibrations in your heart that make you wonder how you ever lost anything, how any connection could have ever been missed. I turned away, remembering Gary. Paul Alcorn looked to be about the same age as him.

"That noise," he asked, catching up to me. "Out of—" he looked at his notes—"Dog Killing Chickens. Is it intentional?"

"The wolf," I said. "I don't know."

"The wolf?"

"Just how I think. A big ghost wolf howling."

"It does sound like that," he said.

We were in the grove. Mammoths Resurrected came into view. Ed'd turned three cars into mammoths, put thick legs and trunks on them, and tusks, and he'd half-buried one so it looked like it was climbing out of the earth, and the second one was leaping like it'd just shook free, and the third was in full run, its trunk raised. From a distance they really did look like mammoths. The rock pile of all the rocks Ed's father and Ed and Gary had picked out of the fields was in the center of the group, and the second mammoth looked like she was leaping over it, her front legs curled up for the leap.

"I don't see how he does it," Paul Alcorn said. "Everywhere you turn, there's something new."

We stood looking at the sculpture, the wind making light scatter through the trees.

"It's like he's trying to bring it all back," Paul Alcorn said. "That's what it feels like. Everything that ever happened here. Everything that's lost, he's trying to retrieve it."

I was too surprised to say anything.

"Even that sound," he said. "The wolf may be howling for them." He nodded at the mammoths. "Or maybe it's the sound of mammoths being born."

It all, together, caught at me—the sound, and what he said, the notion of great animals being born and dying forever, and loss and retrieval, and time crystallizing, all of it echoing. I had to stop walking because I couldn't breathe. I put my hand on Paul Alcorn's shoulder to steady myself and massaged the knot below my rib cage.

"Are you all right?" he asked, genuinely concerned.

I guess you never get over appreciating attention and concern from a young, good-looking man. I nodded, but kept my hand on his shoulder.

"You're not a newstwerp," I said. "That's for sure."

He stared at me for a moment, then burst out laughing. "A newstwerp? Is that what you call us?"

"Ed does. Well, all right, so do I. But you're not one."

"You two aren't what we expected," he said.

"You're not what I expected," I said. "Oliver's close, but you're not." I composed myself, straightened out. "Let's go sit on the rocks."

We walked to the mammoths and sat under the leaping one. It looked more like machine than mammoth close up. Everything Ed made seemed not quite one thing and not quite another, or both at the same time.

"You're right," I said. "About what you said before. There's more to it than just Ed being able to do these sculptures." I'd never talked about this with anyone. I used to bring Gary to this rock pile when he was a toddler and sit in the wind and shade and let him play. It was his favorite place.

"We have a son," I said. "He's a lot like Ed. Too much, I guess. He tried to farm with Ed, but it didn't work. They had a big fight, and Gary just quit. Went off and became a computer programmer. It's never been quite right between them since. Between any of us, really. And this—it's Ed trying to make it up. That's what I think, anyway. But if Ed knew I was telling you this. . . . He doesn't even know it himself."

"How make it up?" he asked.

If he'd said that at all like a reporter, I would have stopped right there.

"Once we're gone, unless there's some reason not to, Gary'll sell this place, and it'll be bought up and bulldozed, turned into another field. Ed's trying to make it a place that can't be just a field. Any artist likes to be paid. Payment for Ed'd be giving Gary a place that he can't sell."

Then I said: "You do your show right, it can happen."

"We don't make the news," he said. "We just report it."

"That's a newstwerp talking," I said. "What gets on Arnie's camera is different than what is, and different than what gets on the news. You make the news, and you know it."

"What about you, Charlene?" he asked.

The mammoth rose over us, and the rocks were hard under me, and time went by all around. "You choose," I said. "If there're sides, you end up choosing whether you want to or not. I want whatever I lost of Gary when I leaned toward Ed. Even if I'd lean that way again."

He thought for a while. "I see," he finally said.

After they left, I didn't know what to do. I picked and washed some lettuce, stood in the house for a while, then went out to the shop. Ed was still welding. When he's in the middle of a piece, he'll forget almost everything else. I opened the door quietly and crept around the bolt bins. The light floated off the end of the rod, crackling and snapping, holding things together and making them new. Ed was running a bead down the entire length of the Packard's hood. I watched as the rod diminished, sinking into and feeding the light. The blue brightness of it filled my eyes. When I saw he was going to change rods, I stepped behind the bolt bins. For a few moments I couldn't see anything, and stood in a strange, bright darkness. Then my sight returned.

When the welding started again, I snuck out of the shop and went down to the cattle tank. Sometimes the ducks would be gathered there, waiting for me, but they weren't this time. In the bright, clear water, strands of algae grew out from the sides of the tank. The wind blew, and I thought I saw the water ripple in the low, ensuing howl. I took off my shoes, then my blue jeans and shirt and underwear, and stepped over the side of the tank.

I slid under. I felt my hair rise and float. The strands of algae drifted out from the sides of the tank and mixed with my hair. I felt them soft and grasping against me. I shut my eyes and heard the underwater hum, wolves and laboring mammoths, and Gary's cry when he was born, and his shouts and Ed's twenty years later, and the crackle and moan of the welder, all mingled and unseparate, while the algae wrapped me up and held me in the sound and cool.

I stayed down until I couldn't anymore. When I rose up, gasping, Ed was standing there.

Algae clung to my neck and shoulders. Strands of it ran down my chest. "Charlene," Ed said, "you do find ways to stay sexy."

"How long you been standing there?" I asked.

"Long enough to wonder should I pull you out."

He would've. But first he waited to see if it was necessary. If you're looking for signs of love, that's not the worst.

"You get to 'em, Charlene?" he asked.

I looked at him. I had, but not in the way he thought. If he knew what I'd told Paul Alcorn. . . . But he didn't. And wouldn't. Maybe the telling and the not-telling both were small betrayals.

"I did, Ed," I said. "I got to them."

"Knew you would," he said.

I held out my hand. "How about you get in?"

"That algae wouldn't look near that good on me."

"Clean and green." I sank under and let it swirl over me, and when I came back up, the patterns on my body were different.

"You think they'll do it right, Charlene?" he asked.

I heard the doubt in his voice tinged far back with fear. Another secret I could keep.

"I know it, Ed," I said.

"Well hell, then." He stepped into the tank, clothes and all, and sank down with me. When he came up, he looked like one of those old drunk gods, with green hair streaking him.

⚛

Paul Alcorn kept his word. The newspiece focused on the sculptures, and it portrayed them well. Oliver Ringburton even got all jumpy like he does when he's enthusiastic. And at the end of the show when they all sit around and pretend that they like each other, Paul Alcorn brought the sculptures up again and encouraged viewers to go see them.

"Think it'll do?" Ed asked when it was over.

"I think so," I said. "We're gonna have people coming out here."

"Gotta take the bad with the good, I guess."

Then the phone rang and kept ringing for a while, neighbors calling, even some that'd thought Ed was sure enough nuts, to say how great they thought it was. Nothing like getting on TV to convince people that something's real.

Ed finally took the phone off the hook. "Let's go outside," he said.

"Where we walking?"

"To the cars."

"The cars? Why there?"

"You'll see."

We walked through the grove, under the quiet trees, and came out in the pasture, where Dog Killing Chickens was moaning loud, and Sacrificial Hawk seemed to be hovering over the grass, the wind moving its large, thin wings, looking like it'd fly away, carrying the boy-figure clinging to its neck with it. We walked over the long pasture grass to the cars. Every car Ed'd ever owned had been junked out here. He never traded—just drove them till they quit, then towed them back here with a tractor. But there were fewer than there used to be.

He led me to an old car seat sitting in front of the junkers like an outdoor couch. "Recognize this?" he asked.

I didn't at first, in the moonlight. Then I touched it and knew. "The Packard," I said.

"The backseat," he said. "I saved it."

"Well well."

"So the Packard's not gone. It's just bigger."

It was as big as the sky. Over by the rock pile, the dark silhouettes of mammoths rose out of the ground, and a little ways away, Old Man Killing Goats seemed to skip and dance. I sat down on the seat, and Ed sat beside me. What you retrieve, I thought, is never quite what you lost. For just a moment my breath caught, and the knot below my rib cage tightened. But I didn't do anything about it. Ed would. There wasn't any hurry. We sat where we sat. After a while Ed touched me, and our hands began to move.

Glacierland

The First Fall: The Rock Surfaces

THE trip mechanism on the plow cracked above the roar of the tractor as the pointed share jammed into granite. The plow rose from the ground like a great broken-winged bird. Steele Hendrickson got down to look.

The gulls kept their distance—white birds from the sea. Steele never knew how they appeared, so far inland. It seemed to him that the ocean could hardly be even a memory for them here, hardly a faint, recalled rhythm. He thought of them floating on foam, high in the water. Here they were graceless and ragged, feeding on insects turned up by the plow.

With his hands, Steele dug into the ground where the share had tripped. He unearthed a hard dome, in color and texture the same as the soil, with a bone-white scar where the hardened point of the share had struck it beneath the surface. He touched the scar, the flinty wound of lanced stone. He could sense the largeness of the rock, could feel it going far into the earth. He felt again, as he so often did, the glacier in the land, massive and implacable.

He thought: *year after year these rocks come up. Year after year I pick them up and dig them out, and still they emerge.*

He knew it was frost that brought them, and erosion. He had heard it was these things. But it didn't seem enough. He touched the scar and felt the rock like a living thing, waiting. Rock blood and rock breath, waiting. He gazed at the gulls rising and settling on bent wings, white on the black soil, and thought of the rock as a great, slow loamfish, moving upward to air and light.

THE PREVIOUS SPRING: CANCER CLAIMS HIS WIFE

Sharon, twenty-five years old, the youngest of the three children and the only girl, hugged her father, then backed away. They looked at each other. Sharon's husband had the car running. Francine's funeral was a week behind them, and Sharon was the last of the children to leave.

"You going to be okay, Dad?"

Steele nodded, his hands in his pockets.

"I could stay with you a while yet."

"No. You need to go."

"What'll you do?"

"What I've always done."

"I suppose." Then: "It's a wet spring, isn't it?"

It was an unexpected question. He looked around. Water was draining from puddle to puddle, quiet and shining in small, eroded gullies in the gravel.

"Wetter than most."

"Remember how I used to dig channels to make this water drain? I'd dig all day, connecting puddles."

"I remember. The puddles were your lakes, and the big one in the driveway ditch was the ocean."

"I wanted all the water to go to the ocean."

"I said it'd never happen."

"You were right."

A shrug.

"You're going to make me go?"

"Go."

She went. The cattle milled around the bunks. Steele fed them, as he always had, then himself in the newly empty house, in a wet April, looking up the empty driveway as he chewed his food.

The First Fall: The Minister Visits

"I suppose you know why I came?"

"I suppose I do."

"You haven't been to church for months. Since Francine . . . since her funeral."

"You been taking attendance?"

"We're concerned."

"We are?"

"Yes. About you. About . . ." In shadow, the minister's hands gestured, helpless as baby-birds' wings.

"My soul?"

The minister wouldn't be baited. "If you want to say that, yes. But we're concerned about *you*, Steele. No one sees you anymore."

"I'm all right."

The windowpane rattled. Looking at it, Steele saw a rectangle of darkness. He remembered the rock. He thought of it out there, as stubborn and silent as when the glacier dropped and buried it. He imagined it at that very moment rising through the earth, coming up from the airless, dark land still carrying the musk of mastodon, the imprint of that long, deep winter.

"Why'd you quit coming to church? You've almost quit coming into Cloten at all."

Steele felt a friendliness for the minister, for the way he did his job. There was something practical and hard-nosed in it, not prying as it had first seemed.

"The question is, why did I go in the first place," he replied.

"Why did you?"

"Francine wanted me to."

"That was the only reason?"

"It was a good one."

"I suppose. And it's not anymore?"

"It was an every-Sunday thing."

"Meaning?"

"Meaning every Sunday she'd ask, and every Sunday I'd say yes."

"And she's not asking anymore."

"She's not."

"Have you lost your faith?"

"I don't think so."

"Because you can't lose what you never had?"

"It's not that."

"What, then?"

Steele shook his head. He stared at the dark glass.

"Time sits out there like a dog," he said. He looked at the minister, ready to stop, but the minister was attentive.

Steele went on. "Francine talked in tongues," he said. "You know that. She knew God like a light in her brain. Never made any sense to me. But it didn't have to. Because if it was real to Francine, it was real to me. I didn't have to understand it. Better if I didn't. But I know God like a rock, Reverend. Maybe that means I don't know Him at all. But I swear sometimes I can smell Him."

He glanced at the minister again, gauging the man's reaction, but the minister simply listened and was silent. Steele turned his face back to the window, stared at it as if he could see through the pane to something beyond it.

"My grandfather wore himself out on this farm," he said. "And my father slipped his disk picking up rocks. Hobbled around, an old man. And every year I go out and continue what they didn't finish. And I won't either. The glacier never leaves this land. I hoist those rocks, and it's like hoisting time. You know what that's like? It's like hoisting God. Time and God weigh a lot, Reverend. They don't fill my brain with light."

He stopped, unused to talking so much.

"I see," the minister said quietly but fervently, as if it were an *Amen!* to a prayer.

Steele was surprised. It gave him courage to go on. "Sometimes I'll pick up a rock out there, and I'll swear I smell the spoor of mammoth. Or in the spring, Reverend, I'll smell the dying in the soil—not a bad smell, but nothing I think anyone could mistake. But Francine'd say, 'No. Smell the breeze. Smell the leaves.' "

THE SECOND FALL: HE MARKS THE ROCK

Steele sometimes imagined the rock like a boil on the land, growing in size and inflammation and tenderness until it seemed that the third year he struck it, the earth winced. He climbed off his tractor then and drove a stake with a red flag on it into the ground near the rock. The gulls, following the plow, engulfed the stake for a while—a red buoy on a fluttering white sea. Then the rear birds flapped up and came to the front, the flock rolling along, until the flag snapped alone in the ongoing wind.

THE SECOND WINTER: A TOUCH OF GLACIER

Christmas holidays ended. Sharon asked: "How long're you going to stay out here, Dad?"

"Since when did it become 'out here'?"

"Don't draw me off, Dad. I worry about you."

"I've got work."

"You're all alone."

"If I get lonely, I'll call you."

Over Sharon's head, through a spot in the frost of the window, Steele saw Caitlin, Sharon's two-year-old, chasing a farm cat. Framed by the frost, she tripped and pitched face-forward into a drift. Steele lurched toward the door. Then the child came back out, bright as when she went in, her nylon suit shedding the powder. She laughed, brushing her face with her mittens, and looked around for the cat.

Sharon jumped up. "Dad! What happened?"

"Nothing. Caitlin fell."

He gazed out the window. The wind knocked snow from the trees in the grove. It came off the boughs in white sheets, thinning and spreading as it fell.

Sharon spoke to his back. "You turned white, Dad."

"I'm not used to kids anymore."

"Dad?"

"You better go. There's a storm coming in. The ground blizzard's starting already."

"Dad, you know, I think I'd go crazy out here alone."

"Maybe that's why you're not living here. You better leave before you can't."

He stood outside in his shirtsleeves and watched them drive away, the snow sticking to his eyebrows and the hair of his forearms.

It was as if the drift had reached up and engulfed the child, then closed again, all in soft silence. Reached up with white arms, too white, and engulfed her.

THE THIRD FALL: A RUSH TO THE LIGHT

Where do gulls sleep when they come inland? In what stationary spot, in what dark wind? After a few rounds with the plow in the morning, they appeared. *From where? What safe place harbored them?*

Steele watched them spread out behind the plow—big birds, white birds, on webbed feet, lifting on easy wings.

He came to the flag. He went around it, then stopped the tractor, shut off the engine, and climbed down in a windy silence. He pulled a spade from the rock box on the tractor, jerked the flag out, and began to dig. The rock grew in size and girth, spreading into the soil, as he went down. The gulls exhausted the life exposed by the plow, then rose in twos and threes, hung in the wind, rose and dropped, and, in twos and threes, flying low, disappeared. Gulls never composed a flock. They arrived in the same place, but coming and going, they were always solitary.

Steele stopped working to watch the last three go. They veered as they flew and seemed always about to go their separate ways, as if their stiff wings, cutting the angling wind, had their own will. Yet they stayed together, lowly, over the fence line. Then they spotted the sky and were gone. Steele returned to his work, casting up the soil in a ring.

The rock emerged, a hard dome in a trench. But it only partially emerged. Steele felt again that it was connected to the core of the earth. With the sun shallow in the sky, he sat on the blunt bulge and watched the wind blow his breath away. He thought of his grandfather, that great-knuckled man of his childhood, riding this rock out of the earth. He thought of his father, eyes always on the ground, and of Francine, eyes closed, hands outspread, head tilted back, incoherent in prayer.

Steele looked at his hands. They were caked, muddy paws, helpless, too heavy to lift from his lap. He felt the rock under him nudging out of the earth. He thought of the years its seconds and the eons its hours, thought of it flaking off soil as a whale, breaching, flakes off water. *If I could see more slowly,* he thought, *I could see the grass grow. More slowly than that, I'd see this rock emerge from the land. And more slowly yet, I'd see it rush to the light. I'd feel its power and thrust. I'd hear the parting of clay.*

THE THIRD SPRING: SOME SORT OF VIOLENCE

Steele was working close to the rock, digging, his shovel often scraping it. The earth seeped. His boots were balls of mud. He dug down until his shoulders were below the edge of the land. The rock continued down, massive, into the earth.

Steele scrabbled up into the wind. Across the field a single white bird cast about in the air. A gull? No: unlikely—the wrong season for gulls. A pigeon, perhaps. From his pickup Steele took a hammer and masonry bit and dropped back into the hole. As he struck the bit again and again, he smelled the acrid tang of burning granite. His shoulders ached. It took a long time. Finally, with the taste of rock dust chalking his mouth, he hoisted himself out of the hole.

He took a stick of dynamite from a small wooden box left over from when it had been legal to buy it. His father had used it for this same purpose. Steele held it, so frail and re-fined, and contemplated the rock exposed to the light. He gazed at it a long time. It didn't move. Didn't pulse or breathe. Steele shook his head. The rock was waiting for nothing. It wasn't swimming upward, carrying the scent of the glaciers that had buried it. It was a boulder that interrupted his plowing. Nothing more.

He walked to the rock, placing his feet steadily on the moist ground. Back down in the trench he stuffed the dy-namite into the holes he'd bored in the rock, attached the fuse, looped it over the top so its weight wouldn't drag it into the water, then climbed back out, thoroughly coated with mud. He uncoiled the fuse, cut it with a jackknife, took matches from his pocket, struck a flame. The fuse sputtered, carrying fire.

Steele stood near the hood of his pickup and watched. That's all he had done when pain had engraved Francine's face, when it had twisted her mouth when she spoke, when it had clenched her hand into a fist and deprived her, finally, of all tongues but its own. He had seen it happen, had watched it happen, the slow degradation, and he had done nothing. Just watched.

The fire circled the rock. Across the field the white bird rose from the ground, cut back and forth in the wind, floating against the pale sky. Steele glanced at it, then back at the sputtering flame. He smelled the purifying hot ash of it—and then, underneath, like something the flame cut a pathway through, the cold, loamy scent of what he'd never, with certainty, named. Startled, he glanced at the white bird again. It was circling as if inside a wind. Steele's old, mute religion gripped him. He lurched around the pickup, slipped in the mud, scrambled to his feet, chasing the receding fire.

"Wait!"

But the flame disappeared down the hole. Steele realized where he was and flung himself facedown in the furrow, into muddy water lying there, reflecting a bit of gray sky. The barely thawed land speared him with its cold.

The air shook.

Wind spread. Rock rained.

Steele struggled to his feet. The white bird was gone. Steele was bruised, cold to his core. Mud dripped from his hair and eyebrows. He stumbled to the hole like a drunk man. The rock was a rubble—shards of the Ice Age. But underneath the rubble lay a still-solid base.

Nothing moved.

Steele backed away, horrified. He sat down on the black

earth, letting the cold soak into his spine. In the bottom of the hole he'd seen water seeping from wounds in the rock.

THE THIRD SPRING: THEY GALLOP AND THUNDER

"Hello, Sharon."

"Dad. What's wrong?"

"Nothing."

"It's three-fifteen in the morning."

"I told you I'd call."

"What?"

"When I got lonely. I told you I'd call."

"Are you all right?"

"Could you come down for a few days? Bring Caitlin?"

"Tell me you're all right."

"I think I've been alone too long. That's all. Things just seem . . ." He didn't finish.

"I'll be there in the morning. You wait for me, okay? I'll bring Caitlin."

"I'll wait."

He hung up the phone. The wind blew against the windows, rose in volume, trumpeted against the siding, as if it would stampede through the house. Steele tried to ignore it. He thought of Sharon coming, in only a few hours, bringing Caitlin, tried to hold that thought. But the wind trumpeted again, and the door moved in the jamb, clattering like dry tusks. Steele went to the door and opened it. The smell of the land, sour, lungwarm, rushed into his face.

He couldn't remember Caitlin or Sharon, not with that wind blowing in his face, not with that smell. He tried to hold their memory, but it went spinning away from him, and then he heard the footsteps, heavy, the creak of huge joints. The night contained great moving shapes, black in the blackness. His grandfather went by, knuckles clenched on a matted mane. Then his father, bent low over a massive, muscular neck. Finally Francine, high above the earth, whispering words that Steele couldn't understand into an ear as large as a door. The wind contained the smell of the herd, manure and oil, and musk frozen for ages, now thawed. Francine babbled again. The mammoths responded. They galloped and thundered. The wind rose to a pitch, to a roar.

The Smell of the Deer

⚜

BEFORE her death, Sara Sinclair became the most bitter woman in this town, so like a nail in the way she regarded the world that she berated the boys who shoveled her walk in the winter for the small patches of snow they missed, accused them of preying on old women, and refused to pay them what she'd agreed to, poking a few musty bills into their palms before shooing them away. The cowed boys retreated up the sidewalk with their scoop shovels never to return, so that in the worst blizzards, snow piled up around Sara's house at the edge of town until her gray shingles appeared as a dirty extension of the drifts. Once or twice some men who'd hunted with her husband, Jerrod, tunneled their way to her door but upon knocking were met by a woman so fierce and thankless, so dried of all human grace, that she might have been the bones and eyes of an owl.

Some of us remembered Sara as a sweet girl who wore

dandelion-chain necklaces and flowers in her hair. We commented on how age changes people. Or marriage does. Jerrod Sinclair came from a strange family, and in the years before he died, he haunted the town park, half drunk by midafternoon, with a voice like the quaver of a stick against a window. He approached young mothers watching their children, lovers holding hands, evening walkers escaping family, and he pinned them down, if he could, with stories of what he'd done in the river valley when he was younger and the valley was wilder.

We never understood why Sara married him, and we never expected the marriage to last. When it did until death, we nevertheless observed that Sara's bitterness and isolation were the end result of marriage to a man who cared for hunting, and later for alcohol, more than he cared for his wife. Satisfied with this easy truth, we left Sara in her snow-muffled house, where she would have been completely alone had it not been for Diane Bourdeaux.

Diane appeared in town one day with her two dogs, the strangest-looking mongrels any of us had ever seen, hungry, lean, orange-gray, looking like some mad mix of greyhound and pit bull—dogs that, though invariably placid, looked like they would enjoy only one thing more than running prey down, and that would be tearing it apart once they caught it. Diane herself was ageless, elegant and earthy both. Her name wasn't German or Scandinavian, and no one knew where she came from. Some said she'd moved to Cloten to work in the gambling hall the Indians had opened in Graniteville, but this was speculation. With her black hair and light brown eyes, her cinnamon skin that even in the winter shone burnished and coppery, and her laugh like sudden bells, she moved among the gullpale folks of Cloten like a mythical bird lost in migration.

It was apparently pure accident that brought her to be Sara Sinclair's caretaker. They met in Aisle 3, Breads and Cereals, of the Red Owl on Diane's first day in town—or at least her first day in the Red Owl. Kenny Christianson, the Red Owl's owner, noticed her pass by the meat counter and decided right then he needed to check inventory. He says she was standing in the middle of Aisle 3 when Sara—then only a few weeks into her widowhood—pushed her cart toward her. Diane, her back to Sara, didn't notice Sara attempt to squeeze through the narrowed aisle next to the cereal boxes and then reach out to move Diane's cart aside.

When Sara touched it, however, the cart lurched around on a wild wheel, transforming itself from a peaceful carrier of groceries into a vicious wire dog. Fluorescent light gleaming off its frame, it attacked the cereal boxes, boring into the shelf with such force that it surprised even Kenny, who knew more about the nature of grocery carts than anyone in Cloten. The cart rammed the shelf with its blunt nose, swept through a good four feet of boxes, then danced to the other side of the aisle, bobbing like a boxer on its uneven wheels, and butted with the force of a battering ram the shelves stacked with Wonder Bread.

The aisle collapsed as if a natural force had hit it. There was a single moment of silence after the last cornflakes box crashed to the tile. Then Diane, unstartled, turned. Her heel scraped the tile. Light glanced off her cheekbone, and Kenny saw her face, stern as a rock, swing around, saw Sara's shoulders collapse under the pitiless eyes, micalike in the grocery-store light, that found her.

But then Diane laughed. None of us had ever heard anything like it in Cloten, though in the few years that Diane stayed with us, we all became familiar with the sound. It was a laugh so infectious, like the music of meadowlarks, under pressure to be happy, that Kenny, owner of the smashed bread, laughed too, and so did the checkers at the front of the store, without knowing what had happened.

The only one in the store not laughing was Sara. We would later say that this was the first sign of her descent into who she became. She gazed at Diane's face for a moment, then turned away, her own face a face of ash. She pushed her cart through the chaos of cereal and past Kenny as if it were a four-legged cane for a cripple, and her eyes, Kenny says, had the hammered look that all of us eventually noticed.

Yet from this inauspicious beginning, Diane became the single person in Cloten who could deal with Sara. Perhaps when she learned of Sara's widowhood she felt guilty for laughing. She visited Sara once—to apologize, we assumed—then visited her again, then again, bringing baskets of fruit and cheese. Neighbors heard Sara shouting, rebuffing Diane's attempts at reconciliation, demanding that Diane "leave me alone!" Anyone else in town—much to our discredit—would have acceded to the demand, but Diane persisted in her friendliness, until finally she was Sara's sole companion. And, as Sara grew more isolated, Diane became her only contact with the outside world, even doing her grocery shopping for her.

We realized just how mysteriously attached Diane had become to Sara when she brought the single pup born of the mating of her dogs into the Red Owl and announced that she was giving it to Sara. "Maybe it'll cheer her up," she said, "having a puppy to take care of." It melted some hearts, though others thought there was something imperious in the way she announced it.

Sara—who had loved all animals when she was a teenager, feeding stray cats and dogs with scraps off her own plate—declaimed more loudly against the pup than against anything else the neighbors could report of her muffled shouts from inside the house including, "Take the bastard away!" and "I don't want the sonofabitch!" Diane left the pup nevertheless.

All of this would mean nothing if it weren't for the unusual way Sara died—so unusual that it made us reassess Jerrod's drunken ramblings. The Sinclairs were one of the oldest families in Cloten. The story goes that when old James Cloten first came to the place that would bear his name, the Sinclairs were already there, as distrustful and secretive as the native animals, and friends only with the Indians.

Jerrod's great-grandfather virtually lived in the river valley, hiking across country to his farm only to sleep with his wife and look in on the resultant children, three sons who took over the farm—such as it was—when he died, and who, like their father, lived more in the valley than in the rundown house guarding its weedy acres. While around the Sinclairs the land began to sprout crops, rich beyond even the immigrants' expectations, the Sinclairs' farm remained a patch of native prairie and scrubby corn. The Germans fought the weeds with a bulldog single-mindedness, and the Scandinavians hunched their huge shoulders to their implements with a strength that rivaled their horses'—but on the Sinclairs' farm the old land held sway, their efforts to subdue it only a nod to convention so that they could return to the mosquito-infested woods.

Into this family Jerrod's father and then Jerrod himself were born. But even the Sinclairs couldn't hold off progress forever. Without their noticing, their land increased in value, borrowing from the neighbors' efforts. Jerrod's father came home from the river one day to find his wife—a thin woman, gray as a dusty leaf—holding an envelope that turned out to be a tax notice asking for more money than the farm had netted that year. Jerrod's father cursed the system and cast himself in the role of savior of the land, ranting that his farm contained the last virgin prairie in the entire county.

However, taxes don't concern themselves with the preservation of species. He had no choice but to sell in order to pay the bill. BigJim Anderson—one of a long line of BigJims, each owning more land than his father—bought the Sinclair farm, bulldozed the ratty house and the tired trees where fox and pheasant escaped winter storms, and loosed his equipment upon it, transforming the virgin prairie into fields to do the work that, in BigJim's eyes, land was meant to do.

Jerrod's father, rather than escaping to the river as we expected, escaped to the bottle, and became a bar regular. His wife divorced him and moved to Clear River, where she married a man who provided her with the luxuries she'd never had. She became obese beyond description, happily settling her great jellylike mass into the wheelchair with which her devoted husband transported her to church. She sighed, content to be pushed up the quiet streets and to remember the bare shack she'd once occupied alone, waiting by the single window for her husband to appear, walking through the wildflowers. Remembering this, she would reach back and place her palm on the sweating hand of her new husband and deliberately jiggle her flesh whenever the wheelchair bumped over a crack, in order to feel the extent of her existence, the flesh she occupied like a queen a kingdom, expanding inexorably, nibbling away at her new husband's resources, taking them into herself.

Then one day she died—perfectly alive, content, and self-satisfied when she left the house, and perfectly dead when she arrived at church, with so little change in her appearance that the four men who helped carry the wheelchair up the church steps stooped over her and grunted in their usual way, speaking lightly about the weather with her husband in order to hide their guilt at how they truly felt about this, their selfless and Christian duty to a God who accepted all weaknesses.

They got her up the sixteen cement steps and to the front pew before one of them detected something he later described as "congealed" about her and tactlessly asked one of his companions, "How do we know she's alive?"—a comment her husband overheard and then remembered she hadn't reached back to touch his hand on the walk to church. He threw himself onto her stupendous bosom, soaking her dress with his tears.

Jerrod, having lost his mother to contentment and his father to bitterness, did what everyone expected a Sinclair to do: he took even more deeply to the woods. Abandoning the shotguns and rifles of his forebears, he killed noiselessly, with a bow, and he treated fence lines—for the valley was just then beginning to be domesticated—as part of the natural world, no more firm in their denial of access than a swamp, which he waded, or the river, which he swam. Landowners could no more prove his presence on their land than they could prove the bobcats and cougar that they also suspected, and soon sign of Jerrod Sinclair became as much a part of local wildlife lore as sign of those elusive cats.

For the few supplies he needed beyond venison and fish, he did carpentry, which he'd been doing even as a teenager, since his father's dissipating when he'd first began living in Ivy Bercovitch's basement. Ivy, a German widow, was Cloten's first landlady. Determined not to be dependent on anyone she turned her cramped basement into an apartment, convinced beyond any reasonable hope that the creation of a rental would create a renter—which, in the small, miraculous way of such things, it did.

Ivy pinned her remaining worries and hopes on Jerrod. When he was gone to the woods, as he usually was, she worried that he might be attacked by wild animals, and when he was in her basement, she worried about his social life and hoped he would marry and have children who would come up the basement steps, surrogates for the grandchildren Ivy'd never had. When Jerrod finally did marry, however, he disappointed Ivy by moving out of the basement and into a house he built at the edge of town, where Sara kept the shades drawn all day and night.

Later in his life, after he, like his father, had taken to alcohol he would sneak up on people in the park, approaching them as silently as he must have once approached other prey, and if they didn't start and run, he would begin telling them stories—or rather, we realized later, perhaps a single story heard in bits and pieces by various people. He would speak in a voice so distant and low that the stories he told seemed distant too, as untouchable as the world spoken by high, gabbling geese.

Because no one heard the entire story—everyone eager

to escape Jerrod's mosquito-insistent voice—it seeped into the town, slow as ice forming at the beginning of winter, built privately and incrementally. It was retold only in quiet places, and never in groups: two men on a boat waiting for a channel cat to find the three-inch sucker dangling in the current below; two lovers watching the moon rise over the river bluffs, whispering the story one of them has heard, a prelude to greater intimacy.

Through such quiet transmission, everyone in Cloten learned the story, but because the moment of hearing it was marked by trust and vulnerability, everyone thought that only two others knew—the person from whom one had heard it, always assumed to have heard it from Jerrod himself, and the one to whom one told it. It was only after Sara's bizarre death that someone flushed the story into the open by asking whether there might be a connection between the two things, death and story.

We all looked at one another then and asked: "You too? You too?" In the cafes, the bars, on church steps after services, we talked of little else, unable to quite believe that everyone knew Jerrod's story. It was as if the whole town woke from a long dream of secrecy, from which we are still waking.

It begins with rain. He'd seen six grown men struggle to lift his mother's casket, and he'd noted, with an eye that would make him the most sought-after carpenter in Cloten, the reinforcing bands that kept her from bursting through the bottom. He left the funeral reception early, put on his hunting clothes, and went to a willow over the river, to stand in a fork within the rain and falling leaves. The river was covered with leaves—brittle, cupped hands, curled inward, holding nothing. He stood for hours, his heart colder than the rain, like a turtle's heart sinking into mud at the bottom of the river.

He grew so still, he said, that he felt as his mother must have felt in that casket, an infinitude of heaviness sinking down. Rain smacked against his camouflaged rainsuit. And then, drifting through the rain came the scents of faraway deer, a buck and three does, like ribbons woven through the trees.

The scent was so strong and distinct that he could picture the animals circling each other as they grazed. He lifted his face to the sky and let the rain fall into it, then climbed down from the tree and set off through the rigid, dead weeds, under the thick hardwood canopy. Night was settling under the trees, filling the cavities alongside trunks. It was too dark for anyone with a conscience to shoot, but he went on anyway, the scent taking him away from the river. He simply wanted to see deer, to watch them graze as night fell: their spindle legs, their nostrils flaring.

For a while he lost the scent, the ribbons sheared by a shifting wind. He waited for the breeze to return, and he remembered the carpentry tools he'd abandoned in Gene Svenson's house, walking out between pounding one nail and the next when Gene had come to him with news of his mother's death. But when the scent returned, he went on.

Then he peered into a triangular clearing at trampled grass where deer had moved and fed. Rain streaked the empty light against a background of gray trees. He walked into the clearing and saw with his practiced eye that deer had recently departed. Grass was dragged into long lines by their hooves. He knelt and touched a hoofprint, the abrupt crescent of it in the earth, then looked around at the hollowness that remains when animals have been frightened off, and thought of bobcat or lion, felt his own back, exposed and bent. But he didn't rise.

The rain turned to snow. Squatting, Jerrod let his eyes drift upward against the descending flakes. His spine felt bowed and taut, as if one touch of a claw would rupture it and his body would fly like a broken spring across the clearing. His eyes sought yellow eyes, a furred and whiskered face. He focused on a fork in a tree where something seemed unnecessary, a concentration of foliage or an outgrowth of bark. He stared until he realized he was looking into a pair of eyes that stared back at him.

Jerrod should have been startled. He noticed the brownness of the eyes first, and then the curled lashes and the brows shaped and arched. The rest of the face faded into the trees. He should have been startled, but he'd been expecting yellow eyes with slits that regarded him as prey, and these brown eyes, though unexpected, were merely appraising.

Without rising, he said, "You scared them away."

The eyes blinked.

"You scared them away," he repeated.

Lips formed. "You saw me," they said.

"Why'd you scare them away?"

"How did you see me?"

"I looked," he said tersely.

He saw a smile and then the tip of a tongue behind white teeth. Only then was he startled.

"I didn't want you to shoot," she said, finally answering.

Though it was freezing in the clearing, the backs of his hands felt warm.

"I wasn't going to shoot."

She disappeared for a moment; then she was on the ground, moving over the damp grass. She stopped in front of him.

"Men usually shoot."

Jerrod had never met a woman bow-hunting before. He glanced at the bow she carried lightly in her left hand, an ancient thing. He'd never seen camouflage like hers, a pattern that made her face seem without surface, made it, even close up, part of the background. He listened for the sound of someone else in the woods, a man who accompanied her, but the falling snow made the only sound.

She knew what he was thinking. "No," she said. "I'm quite alone."

It seemed a brazen statement. Too confident. A challenge. He was twenty years old. Too young to think of himself as a dangerous man. Too young, almost, to think of himself as a man. Yet he suddenly felt dangerous. Or—he wasn't sure— in danger. To keep the thoughts at bay, he asked, "What are you doing here?"

A shadow of irritation passed over her face. "What are you?"

"Of course. Yes." What would anybody be doing but hunting? "Have you seen many deer?"

She gazed at him, her eyes brown as oak leaves before they fall. He turned from her gaze to the falling snowlines, the dripping trees, the closing dark—but in spite of his look- ing away, it seemed to him that the death of his mother, and his father's desertion, and the orphaning off of his land had all been for this: that he would climb the willow and smell the deer and come to meet her and want her, this woman, here in the danger of snow.

"How did you know there were deer here?" she asked.

"I smelled them. A buck and three does."

He had the courage to meet her eyes again. She smiled. Her teeth were white as the snow that now formed a layer over the grass and seemed to be the sole source of remaining light. She laid her bow on the ground and rose and took his head in her hands. For a moment he thought to jerk away like a wild animal, but her lips touched his, and he smelled the sweet grass she had chewed to scent and disguise her breath.

So it is said.

They lay next to each other, on their clothes. Jerrod stared upward into a darkness so deep he couldn't see the snow falling onto his face and body. Next to him the woman lay still, her skin unnaturally warm against his. He wondered if he were in a delirium of winter, dreaming of her heat.

Her joints slid past each other as she rose. He groped for his clothes and was surprised to smell the four deer again in the woods outside the clearing, standing under the dark trees damphaired, a smell like old, wet paper. Then her sweet smell rose out of the scent of the deer. He opened his arms. She stepped into them. Shivering, he pulled her in.

"I've got to go now," she said.

"I'll come with you." He had no past to return to.

"No."

"Why not?"

He thought that his reasons were hers, that she too had no past, that their lovemaking had given them the same future.

"Sweet boy," she said. In all versions of the story, through whichever channel it flowed, these words are the same.

Sweet boy.

He couldn't imagine any man containing her, any more than he was able to contain her as she slipped from his arms and he felt cold air fill the space next to his skin. Yet he couldn't imagine why she would leave him if not to preserve a past, and he was struck by jealousy for the man who wasn't here. He stepped toward her but couldn't find her.

"Is there someone else?" he called, groping for her. "Will I see you again?"

"It all depends." Her voice came from a distance, but he didn't know which question she answered, if she answered one at all.

His total disappearance into the woods was hardly noticed. Gene Svenson complained about his unfinished wall, while his wife Ruthie berated him for hiring a Sinclair. And Ivy Bercovitch heard in her house the same silence she'd heard after her husband died, and she told her plants that her tenant had fallen hard, either for a woman or for the bottle—those quiet types fell hard either way. Unable to decide which it was, Ivy prayed prayers of thanks in the morning for the children who might soon grace her upstairs rooms, and in the evenings, having fretted all day, she prayed that Jerrod might be delivered from the amber curse.

The weather warmed again, the early snow melted, and the woods glowed with orange light. Beginning always in the willow along the river, Jerrod made his way through the burdock and preacher's lice and wild hemp to the clearing. He carried his bow but never shot. If he saw deer on the trails that wound like faint threads through the undergrowth, he watched them go by.

She was always waiting for him, concealed next to a trunk, or higher up where the branches thinned and multiplied. It was always her eyes that he saw first. She taught him all the ways of love, her knowledge greater than his imagination, until the clearing grass was pressed flat, like a deer's bedding area. She told him that she had watched countless men go by who had never seen her, men who stared right at her and didn't see, men who smoked tobacco within two feet and gazed through their own cloud at her face and didn't see. Jerrod didn't care if she was lying or telling the truth; he had seen her, and she was his.

One day he opened his eyes as they were making love and found the buck and does grazing around them, unperturbed. The sight stilled and awed him, their bodies joined and the animals accepting them, content to graze. "Look," he exclaimed.

And the whole town of Cloten, in different places and situations—some yearning, some horrified; some disbelieving, some awed; some drunk, some sober; some staring into darkness, some staring into light; but all of them in pairs: man and woman, adult and adolescent, friend and friend—all of them look, and willfully or in spite of their will, see what Jerrod wishes his lover to see: the four deer accepting their lovemaking.

He reached out to touch her face, from which she had never removed her camouflage. He had given up ever seeing her face for the same reason he'd given up knowing her name—because he thought she protected another life outside the woods, something domestic and calm. But now she kissed his palm as he ran it over her cheek. Then she stood and went to her quiver, opened a pouch and took out a small cloth. She brought this and her canteen back to him and knelt in front of him and poured water on the cloth and held it out.

He touched her face with it. A drop of water rolled down her cheek. He washed the camouflage off. It was, he said, the tenderest thing he'd ever done, the two of them kneeling together, her nostrils dilated as she breathed with shut eyes. The camouflage streaked at first, the colors mixing to form muddy gray lines that ran down her neck, streaked her shoulders and breasts. Jerrod rinsed the cloth in the water from the canteen, wiped the streaks off. He cleaned her brow, washed her cheekbones.

Without opening her eyes, she said: "You've seen my face now."

"Yes," he said. "You're beautiful."

"I am," she said—as if beauty, for her, were fact.

The long Indian summer ended. She stood in his arms one evening, both of them wrapped in the same blanket.

"There'll be snow in the morning," she said. "Staying snow."

"How do you know?"

"This is the last evening."

"The last evening for what?"

"We can't come here in the winter."

"We'll meet in town somewhere."

"That's not possible. We have to wait until spring."

He pled with her. Her eyes turned hard. She walked away from his pleading into the woods, promising impatiently to return in the spring, when the snow had melted. He stood in the clearing, forbidden to follow her while dry trees clattered about him. He felt her absence turn in his chest like tumbling and shattered glass.

He showed up at Gene Svenson's the next day and in a grim precision of loss, picked up the hammer where he'd left it lying, and the eight-penny nail he'd dropped back into his pouch, and with one blow drove the nail below the surface of a two-by-four. Working nonstop like this for thirty-six hours, he finished the entire remodeling Gene and Ruthie had asked for. After the first twelve hours, Ruthie complained, and Gene went to Jerrod and suggested that maybe he'd think of quitting—beings as how they'd waited this long for the room, there wasn't so much urgency to all of a sudden finish it. Jerrod turned and looked at Gene. Periodically throughout the night Gene tried to tell Ruthie about that look, both of them listening to the incessant hammer and whining saw.

"It was like a lake looks just after the ice's melted—but like it had ideas to drown you, Ruthie. You wouldn't argue with that, would you?"

"I would if it was in my house."

But Gene, having actually seen the look he couldn't describe, ignored Ruthie's implication of cowardice.

"It ain't, Ruthie," he said. "Not your house again till he's finished and gone."

When he had finished and gone, Jerrod returned to the basement apartment. Ivy, staring through the window, said a prayer of thanks. For a few months, as winter deepened and snow swept across the frozen fields, filling the valley with snowdrifts five and six feet deep, Jerrod entombed himself in Ivy's basement. No one saw him except for the checkers at the Red Owl. Maude Grabow, an old woman now, says he looked like death warmed over, coming in sporadically for a few groceries, smelling of mildew and damp places.

Sara Jacobson was working in the Red Owl then, a sixteen-year-old girl too gentle, almost, for life. She wept when her father sold cattle, and she could hardly bring herself to touch the packets of meat wrapped in white paper that customers laid on her belt at the store. People with too many kittens or puppies, and too little fortitude, dropped them off near the Jacobson place. Sara found them and adopted them all, to her father's exasperation.

Why such a girl would be attracted to a Sinclair, hunters without qualm for generations, is a mystery. But Jerrod had the look of a lost puppy in the weeks before Sara spoke to him, and Maude Grabow believes Sara couldn't resist this look. She had to talk to him when he came through her line, had to reach out furtively and touch his hand when she took the few crumpled bills he held out, and meet his eyes and smile shyly.

And Jerrod?

There is only this in the various remnants of his story: one night, in the middle of a blizzard, he heard a tentative knock on the door at the top of the steps, and he went up, thinking that someone was looking for Ivy at the wrong door. He found Sara Jacobson there, capless, her hair spraying about her face in the wind, her cheeks flushed red, a denim barn coat pulled to her chest with crossed arms.

"I was on my way home," she said. "I saw you in the store again today, and I thought I'd see . . ."

Then the confidence dropped out of her voice, the casual lie shattered by the eyes that gazed at her, and the hand that floated up and took hers to lead her down the dark steps.

⟁

For three months they lived together in Ivy's basement. Sara's parents, though distraught, had long ago given up trying to influence their strange daughter, made willful by her own gentleness. And Ivy Bercovitch, though she fretted, couldn't bring herself to kick them out, her hopes that a child might be conceived overcoming her Lutheran morals.

Then, on a spring morning, Jerrod woke from a dream of the last snow in the woods melting, turning transparent in the sun. Sara lay in bed beside him, and he touched her shoulder, knowing that in spite of her love, he would betray her— though he had been surprised by the possessiveness in her otterlike body, the hunger there, as if she would save him by her fierce abandon.

When he woke her and told her he was going to the woods, she asked: "To hunt?"

He sensed a fight bubbling under the surface. He could see the set of her jaw, a stoniness about her mouth, her stubbornness hardening. She might demand he choose between hunting or her. He didn't have time for justification. Or for choice. Or truth. He shrugged her away.

"Just to go," he said.

The woods smelled of sap rising and animal droppings thawed. His heart loosened like the sweep of the river flooding open fields. He breathed deeply, forcing the basement air that he and Sara had shared out of his lungs. Dulled from the first winter he'd ever spent entirely in town, he didn't smell the deer until he was almost in the clearing. He entered it and found her among the deer—his lover, watching him, there as she'd promised.

He returned to the basement at one in the morning. Sara, alone and awake, heard his foot on the step. The door to the apartment opened silently. Jerrod had taken the door off its hinges and run a graphite pencil over the hinge posts, coloring them gray, and when he replaced the door, it was noiseless. But air moved on Sara's face, and she knew Jerrod stood in the doorway. He stepped into the room; she could see him in the few rays of light coming through the small window from a distant street lamp. Without rising or moving, she said: "Talk to me, Jerrod."

He walked, unnervingly silent, to the bed and sat down. He took her hand. Until he touched her, he might have been a wild animal stalking toward her in the dark.

"What is it?" she asked. "Talk to me."

"It's the river," he said. "The valley."

She waited for him to go on. He looked away, at the shadows cast by the thin light onto the back wall. Even though he was betraying her, he wanted her to know something of his passion. He thought of when it had all started, the rain in the willow, the river full of brittle hands.

"I've been going to the valley all my life," he said. "Before my mother died. Before we lost the farm. There's a willow by the river. If I sit in it, so still that squirrels think I'm part of the tree and run up and down me—if I stay that still, Sara, I'll smell deer."

Sara gasped. She jerked her hand to her mouth and half-rose from the bed, choking, her face working.

His heart sank, that she'd intuited the truth.

Then he realized she was gazing past him.

He turned. A shadow moved across the back wall as he did, in the sweep of a passing automobile's headlights, and something clattered on the street, and a wind from nowhere gusted hard against the house.

Sara pointed to the narrow, low window of the basement. But it was blank, a dark glass to the night.

"What? There's nothing there."

Her mouth worked. Her throat convulsed. When she met his eyes, his hair stood on end.

"There was," she whispered. "A deer. When you were talking. Looking at us."

In the morning he returned to the woods. Sara begged him to stay. He told her she might have seen a dog, and so what if it was a deer, they wander through town sometimes.

"No," she said. "It wasn't like that. It was watching *us*."

She told him she wouldn't be there when he returned. If he was going to live in the woods, she wouldn't wait for him. Even as he walked up the steps she was putting her things—a few of her father's shirts, some jeans—into a small bag, to return to her parents' farm.

In the clearing the woman waited, while the four deer that had grown accustomed to Jerrod grazed around her. Jerrod watched them carefully but saw nothing unfamiliar about them. They were wild animals living wild, alert only to the woods.

He reached for his lover.

She stepped away from him.

"You betrayed me." He'd never heard so cold a voice.

Yet he never knew, as would be repeated in all the story's manifestations through all the years, whether it was a statement or a question. It was as if, in telling the story again and again, he was trying to capture the precise intonation and so know what had been said.

"Betrayed you?"

"I asked you to wait a winter. That's all I asked."

He didn't deny Sara to her. He lost his one chance to deny Sara, and as he would say later—the only moral he ever offered—there is only one chance, ever, for denial, momentary as a whirlwind, and if missed, gone forever.

"I didn't know," he said desperately. "I didn't know what to think."

He stopped, sensing how little the words would clutch and hold what he intended them to say, how they would turn against themselves and speak what would seem a lie—that he'd betrayed her because he loved her, and in her absence didn't know what else to do. A truth—but if spoken it would seem cheap and empty.

"If I ever see your face again—she hissed like fire consuming drought-killed grass—I'll kill you. How dare you betray me? I showed you my face, and you think you can *betray* me?"

And she turned and was gone, swallowed by the woods.

For weeks he drifted through the valley, as he'd drifted after he lost the farm, and again after seeing his father glassy-eyed, who'd once been keen with a rifle. He felt as if his life were being taken from him piece by piece, even as he found and gathered it. We forgot that he existed, made of him a wild thing, the last denizen of the valley, more mythical than the cougar and bobcats that had become mere sign and spoor told of.

Only Ivy waited for him. And Sara—doing her daily routine at the checkout counter of the Red Owl, passing desultory items through her listless hands. Perhaps her waiting drew him back, and Ivy's ungrounded and ridiculous love. Or perhaps the intractable silence of the valley forced him back. In any case he appeared in the Red Owl one day and wandered through the store, plucking from the shelves a single can of coffee. He carried it to Sara's checkout lane and laid it on the belt. She didn't look up. She stated the price in a monotone.

"Sara," he said.

Her hand rested on the keys of the cash register. She stared at her fingers there.

"You want the woods, stay there," she said.

She looked small, drowning in a shirt too large for her. He reached out and placed a diamond ring on the coffee can. It was his mother's ring, from her marriage to his father. She had given it to him a few months before she died, the ring tiny in her overgrown hand.

"If we still had that farm," she'd said, "I'd never give you this. You'd be just like your father—haul a girl out there and forget her. But it's a curse gone from your life. Praise the Lord, son. You find a good girl, you give her that ring. Settle down in town. Make her happier than your father ever made me. Make that ring worth something."

Sara looked at the ring on the can of coffee.

"Why should I, Jerrod?"

He looked around as if he'd just discovered where he was and found it incomprehensible—the magazines on the rack, the paperback books, the candy, the large window, the great red owl with pointed ears and hollow, friendly eyes overseeing all the aisles from its vantage on the front wall.

"I don't know, Sara," he said. "If you need a reason, you probably shouldn't."

❧

He tried to do as his mother had instructed. He built Sara the house at the edge of town, the way she wanted it built and better than she knew, with seams so tight and alignments so true that nothing ever loosened in it, no nail ever budged. It still stands, empty now but refusing to decay.

Jerrod applied himself to carpentry, deserted the woods. He grew rich in the way of small-town riches, nothing ostentatious but more than enough. But neither work nor possessions nor Sara nor the dogs and cats she still attracted and fed could drive the unknown woman from his mind or dreams. He tried to push her out with the nails he pounded, or excise her with the saws that snarled through the fibers of wood, but at night she resided in him, oak-leaf eyes that watched him sleep.

Three years after he married Sara, he woke one fall night from a dream where he had clearly seen the pattern of the camouflage the woman had worn to hide herself. He woke remembering each line and shading, each weave of color. He smelled rain outside and put on his robe and went into it, stood under the maple in the yard and let the water-weighted leaves fall onto his hair, and he felt with a certainty that rooted him till the sun rose over the fields outside of town, where the corn was standing brown to be harvested, that without a death, the heart can never be certain of its losses.

He walked into the house and took his bow off the wall, where it had gathered a thick layer of dust. When Sara woke, he was at the kitchen table, sharpening broadheads.

"What are you doing?" she asked.

"I'm going hunting. It's time I did it again."

She poured orange juice, stood with her back to him for a moment, then turned.

"How can you do it?"

"Do what?" The razor edges barely missed his fingers.

"How can you shoot arrows into animals? I hate the thought of it."

He stopped sharpening. He remembered how his mother used to fight with his father over this. He'd hated those fights. He'd sided with his father, and he hated his mother's unreasonableness, her certainty of moral rightness. She'd never wanted to understand; even as a child, he knew that.

But Sara wasn't his mother. And she loved him. He could see it in her beautiful face, made slack by the sorrow of incomprehension.

Still, he made no attempt to console or help or even to fight her.

"Quit eating then," he said. "Plants, animals. One way or the other, something dies. You don't like it, starve."

He'd never hurt her like that. He saw a dull, glazed coating of shock in her eyes, a look like galvanized metal.

He went into the bathroom and shaved his face smooth. He remembered the woman's face, the camouflage applied so perfectly that he saw only the eyes, the rest of the face like light turned off a leaf, or shadow in a leaf crease. He began to copy onto his own face the image of hers, applying old camouflage paint that he hadn't used for years in fits and starts of correction, until he heard Sara leave the house for work, speaking quietly to the dogs and cats, petting each one. He stopped for a moment to listen, then when the door shut, went on with the camouflage, until staring out of the mirror was the face of the woman as he'd first seen her, his own face, hardly a face at all.

Out of sight of the clearing, he dropped to his hands and knees, then to his stomach, sliding his bow forward. He moved through the preacher's lice and wild hemp like a snake, parting the stems with his body. It took him most of the morning before he saw the clearing through the weed stems.

Within it, the four deer grazed, raising their heads to the wind. He inched back into the trees until he came to a large oak, and behind it, he stood.

He backed into the shadow of the trees until he was looking down a narrow passageway between trunks. He waited, more still than the trunks he stood among. One of the does grazed into the lane, grazed out, in the careless time of animals, while the sun moved in the sky and the faraway river flowed, and leaves dropped out of trees. He heard the muffled clacking of his heart valves inside his chest.

A twig appeared in the lane. Still he didn't move. The twig came farther, forked. Only then did he slowly raise the bow, letting it drift upward as if on a slow breeze, and he drew back the string to the corner of his mouth as the buck's rack, lowered for grazing, moved forward along the ground. The deer's head and shoulders appeared, then its rib cage. Jerrod centered the thin line of sharpened steel there.

The buck took one more step. It raised its head. Jerrod Sinclair would later say it looked down the lane at him with an expression human and sensible, and quizzical, looked at him in the shadows with drawn bow, motionless. And he would repeat again and again that the buck knew him. Not only saw, but knew. And knew what he was doing. And yet merely waited.

He released the arrow.

It glittered and spun light, arcing down its flattened parabola through the line of trees. It disappeared into its own thinness. The buck took a step forward, a second. Jerrod's heart leaped with exultation and disappointment, whirled in his chest like an out-of-round wheel, that he had missed, that his decision had been stolen from him.

Then the buck plunged.

And only at the last moment, as its knees buckled and its head snapped forward to strike the ground, its long neck like a curling whip, and one of its antlers cracked with the force of the fall—only then did it take its accusing and compassionate eyes off the spot where Jerrod stood.

Even the leaves stopped moving, he said.

He waited for her scream.

None came.

Remorse deepened in his heart like thick mud filling it.

He walked into the clearing, but before he entered it, he turned down his face.

The buck shed its heat in great waves. Jerrod stood within that heat, breathing it, his tongue dried stiff and thick in his mouth. He knelt and touched the animal's coarse hair. He looked into its eyes, so dead they didn't even reflect him kneeling there.

He sank further into the grass until it rose around his face. He slowly turned his head and he heard a folding of cloth as he did. His heart beat hard under the shining point of the arrow he felt centered on it.

Then he turned his face full on the spot where the sound came from. He found her even as she screamed at last, in rage and disbelief. "If I ever see your face," she'd said. And he knew, even as he found the brown eyes that burned out of a shifting, blurry space that those eyes saw only the same thing—his eyes floating, not part of a face seen, but peering like part of the earth from the ground itself.

She'd been tricked. She shrieked, a sound worse than a great tree splintering. He saw, with a yearning too large for his heart, her white teeth, her tongue. But his blood went cold at her inhuman shriek. He tried to call to her, but the heat of the dead buck had dried his tongue to a stick.

That was the story he told—or the story we put together out of whatever it really was he told, which may have been nothing more than the rags and scraps of a drunk rummaging through his memory. When he gave up his hunting and then his carpentry and followed his father into the bottle, we thought it was nothing more than the way of the Sinclairs, which may still be a truer view than any explanation offered by the things he said. If it hadn't been for Sara's odd death, none of us would have attached anything but personal meaning to what we knew.

One day he simply disappeared, didn't return home in the evening. Some men who had known him when he was younger came to Sara's aid. They crowded into her living room to plan a search. Sara no longer kept animals, perhaps because keeping Jerrod was mercy enough, but the house still smelled faintly of their years-old presence.

"Where do you think he might have gone?" one asked.

Sara gazed at him. He felt like a bad student.

"The river," she said tiredly. "Where else?"

They searched the valley and eventually found his car. Starting from there, they combed all the wild places they knew. Unsuccessful at the end of the day, they returned to Cloten and insisted to Sara's gray face that they'd looked everywhere.

"No," she said. "You haven't."

The next morning they returned. A new snow had fallen overnight. All morning they puffed through the woods calling. Finally one of them, walking from one patch of woods to another across a field of cornstalks long cleared of trees and fenced now, saw snowblurred tracks and followed them. He found Jerrod's frozen body, naked, clothes scattered about, lying within an area trampled by deer. An empty bourbon bottle lay nearby.

Local wisdom held that freezing people, their delirious

minds deprived of oxygen, often tear off their clothes as blood rushes to their skin, making them feel hot, and alcohol only makes it worse. The editor of the local paper, in fact, followed the story of Jerrod's death with an article about the warning signs of hypothermia and freezing—a bit tactless many of us thought, but certainly to the point.

The only real dissenter in this opinion was Ivy Bercovitch, by now an ancient resident of the Cloten Manor, who spent her days staring out the big picture window of the manor at the field across the highway. She wrote a letter to the editor, a nearly incoherent thesis of paranoia, that was nevertheless printed. Ivy's point—if she had one—was that strange forces operated in the woods, disguising themselves to seem innocuous, and that she'd always known that her old tenant would be taken by them.

Then Sara died. And our horror at the way she died has left us with no certainties. It wasn't just the way she died; it was that none of us did a thing to prevent it. We let a stranger take over a job we should have done ourselves, even if Sara was cantankerous and difficult. We were too happy to let Diane Bourdeaux make our lives easier.

For a year and a half she was Sara's caretaker. She became part of the routine of the town—her weekly visits to the Red Owl, her dogs that followed her around and played with the children, her laughter at the smallest things, her glowing skin, bright eyes. We forgot she was a stranger.

One week, in an already cold winter, the biggest blizzard many of us could remember struck, a white-out that lasted three days and confined us all to our houses except for the farmers who had to feed their livestock. Snow fell so hard and heavy it came down in long, solid ribbons that unfurled on the ground—sheets of snow, planes of snow.

And the wind. We'd never heard such wind. It came from all directions at once, shrieking with a sound that battered at our sanity as we huddled in our houses. It knocked down power lines, leaving the entire town without electricity for the three days of the blizzard and the two following it.

Sara's house disappeared, which was one of the reasons we forgot about her, along with the fact that she'd been gone from our lives for so long. Her house had turned into one large drift that blended with Earl Jensen's field—a big drift, true, but there were big drifts everywhere. We just didn't stop to remember that there was a house under that drift. It was a place that for a few days ceased to exist, a blank spot in the geography of our memories.

It wasn't until three days after the blizzard that Kenny Christianson looked up from the meat counter, puzzled— and then realized that he expected to see Diane Bourdeaux coming toward him on her weekly shopping trip for Sara, buying cereal, bread, fruit, dog food for the now-grown pup.

Kenny walked into the aisles, his head buzzing like the fluorescent lights above him, astonished at the emptiness of the store. Only then did he think of Sara.

We tunneled in, blindly, not even sure where her door lay.

We found it, entered.

Only the pup greeted us, fawning, licking our faces, whining with joy over our attention and the chance to finally escape the closed-in house.

"Sara?" we called, but she didn't answer.

We found her on the bed.

What was left of her.

Men whose faces the pup had licked washed for days, and their wives refused for a long time to kiss them.

The coroner claimed she'd frozen to death first. Who could blame the pup? There was no food in the house. There was nothing at all.

Once we recovered from our shock, someone thought to shoot the dog. Then we discovered it was gone. We'd left the door open a crack, wedged by snow, and the pup had escaped while we gazed in horror at the exposed bones and chewed flesh of what had been, when younger, the beautiful face of Sara Sinclair. There were reports of a dog as large as a deer streaking across farmland toward the river, its body curling and straightening like a steel leaf-spring over the frozen clods of plowed earth.

That—again—might have been the end of it. Except that someone got to thinking about what he'd heard of Jerrod's story, and he brought the story into the open. Then we all looked at one another as if waking from a dream. And since then, none of us has figured out where any of this ends, or where it started, or whether the whole thing is a single story, or two, or more than we can count.

Abiding by Law

T HE old man next door started killing goats again, right
in the middle of *Lucy*. The bleating and babbling
through the screen door made me miss a punch line, and since
Geraldine died and I retired, I can use any laugh I can get.
Those people—over to Clear River, I hear they've been snar-
ing geese from the power-plant lake, don't see nothing wrong
with it, big hunters, hey, what a country, they warm the water
here to tame the birds and make the hunting easier.

I didn't personally have nothing against them coming here
to Cloten, even if it was the Lutherans brought them in.
When the Lutherans first started fixing up the house next
door, no one heard me complain. I turned up the TV and
figured the sound of a Skil saw's the sound of progress. I was
all for the new cable system in town, too, though some said
what do we need cable for, we got the tower over to the
Graniteville cemetery, gets us three stations just fine and we

don't have to pay for it unless we feel like it. I hate that kind of attitude. I pay for everything I get. Anyway, I said Cloten's got to progress, and that system proved me right. I can watch *Lucy* or *My Three Sons* or *The Honeymooners* on the rerun stations any time I want, don't have to put up with that modern crap with smart-aleck kids and aliens.

So when they arrived and the Lutherans moved them in, I didn't say nothing, just watched out my window during commercial breaks. And when they put up the fence, I didn't say nothing either. I'm not one to tell people what they can do with their own property. Even when they moved the goats in, I thought live and let live. I was the only one around could see them over that fence out my second-story window, and a few goats in town, what the hell. Lyle Nordstrom's hog operation a mile away smells worse, and the only ones ever complain about it are the ones who came here and bought houses figuring to make a killing when the Indians put the casino in up to Graniteville.

But the first time the old man killed a goat, I didn't know what to make of it, all that wheezing and thumping and thudding. The second time, I went upstairs to see over the fence, and there stood the old guy, blood on his forearms, even got blood on his little white beard, looking pleased as all get-out, and this goat kicking its legs—kick, kick, kick—a little circle with its back leg raising dust on that lawn that's turned to nothing but dirt the way they take care of it like they never heard of water, and those goats pulverizing it. The old guy let that kicked-up dust float around him, until the blood on his arms and bare, scrawny chest turned from red to brown same as the rest of him, the way my grandkids last time I saw them, Katy and Sam, got into some mud and were having a great time till Sandy their mother came back and had a fit and then chewed me out for not watching them good enough—as if dirt ever hurt a kid—and Karl Junior agreed, didn't even stick up for me, and then they left early, back to Minneapolis.

When the goat got done kicking, the old guy bent down and kind of bowed to it, like congratulating it for a good die. Then he gathered its legs up—I don't know how a guy so scrawny managed it—and swung that dead goat onto his shoulder and marched to this piece of plywood laid out on a couple sawhorses. I quit watching then, figured there were some things I didn't need to see. I went downstairs and made myself a Spam sandwich and watched *The Beverly Hillbillies*, Geraldine used to love them, Jethro so stupid and Granny so ornery, while I thought what to do.

I considered calling the Lutheran minister and telling him to get his holy ass over here, but when I thought how the old guy had picked that goat up without even letting go his knife, I didn't figure the Lutheran minister would have much effect. I climbed back upstairs and looked out the window again.

This time the kid was with the old guy. The old guy pointed and faked like he was cutting, then handed the knife to the kid and talked and pointed some more. The kid looked pretty sullen. He was good at that; when he first moved in, I thought he was about as sullen a kid as I'd ever seen, slouching into the house. He took the knife from the old man like it had something evil on its handle, and he made the cut the way the old man showed, but like he had wood in his joints—the way Karl Junior used to act when I made him learn something he couldn't see the worth of knowing, back when he was wise.

I decided if the old guy was passing down his goat-killing skills to the kid, I'd be listening to goats dying till I kicked off myself—not how I wanted to spend retirement. So I went to the next Town Council meeting to raise a ruckus about it. Turned out there wasn't no particular law in Cloten against killing goats. I figured no big deal, I'd get one, but there was way more discussion than I thought. All sorts of points were raised, and the motion was tabled.

Then word got around, and all the deer hunters, who invade the river valley with shotguns and slugs in the fall and make a massacre of the deer for a few days, they showed up at the next meeting, saying how if a law like this got passed, they wouldn't maybe be allowed to hang their deer up by the neck from a tree limb to age before they butchered it. Every fall this town has deer hanging all over the place. You drive through at night and your headlights go into the yards. It can be pretty spooky, all those bulky shapes swaying in the breeze, with heads hanging down, and eyes. Geraldine used to hate it, wouldn't go into town during deer season—we were still farming then—but that's the way it is if you live here. Some people complain every year, but most just figure it's always been done that way, part of the traditions here, good or bad. The deer get replaced by Christmas decorations as the season changes.

I didn't myself think it'd be so bad not to have those deer hung up, but I could see the deer hunters' point. Then some people got to wondering if we wanted to be like Sioux Falls, where nobody could do anything without a permit. What would this town be like then? Then Hardell Chatham pipes up with how about angleworms. If you got a law against killing goats, might not somebody—that's the way he put it;

might not somebody—apply the precedent to keep you from digging angleworms for fishing? Or how about spraying tomatoes for bugs, he says—introducing poisons into the environment, we sure don't want to make that illegal.

People pretty much let Hardell talk because he likes it so much and then ignore him. I stood and said: "Look. All I want's a law against killing goats. All this other stuff, I don't care about. You're my neighbors, and I'm asking for help—so how about it?"

That got them quiet, but Hardell pretty soon came back with: "Seems they're your neighbors, too, Karl. Why not go ask *them* would they mind not killing goats, especially when a good show's on?"

"Hardell, I'm not even sure they speak English," I said. "How'm I gonna talk to 'em?"

"My mother used to say, 'How do you know unless you try?' " Hardell replied.

Now we had Hardell's mother getting in her two cents' worth. "Look," I said to Fred Wilson, the mayor. "Just a simple law against killing goats. How hard's that?"

Turned out to be another council-meeting hard, but it finally got done. When it came out in the newspaper, I stuck it on the refrigerator where I could read it. My law. Five days later what happens but I'm watching *Lucy* like I said, and the old guy up and kills another goat.

Which just proved, of course, that Hardell and his idea of talking was a crock. It was obvious we needed a law, since the old guy had just broke it now. *All right,* I thought—*when someone breaks a law, I know what to do.* Just like when Karl

Junior'd break a law I laid down, there wasn't no doubt in my mind how to deal with it.

I dialed Debbie up downtown and told her to get the sheriff. Cloten's not big enough for its own cop, so we contract with the county sheriff. "We got a goat-killing, Debbie," I said, "and there's a law against it. So get the sheriff down here to do his job."

Response time isn't real fast. I went up to the second floor to watch the progress of the crime. Luckily the old guy was giving the kid another lesson, turning him into a criminal too, and slowing down the disposal of the evidence. The kid wouldn't take the knife, though, stood with his hands in his pockets and seemed to be arguing with the old guy, while the old guy waved and sliced the air and pointed.

I expected any moment, the way the kid was acting, that he'd pretty soon yell and stamp away, big, dusty, dramatic exit like Karl Junior used to give me, but instead he just stood there, talking. I couldn't stand it after a while, all that action and nothing happening, and I went back downstairs.

I looked out the front window and there was Hardell Chatham parking at the curb. I walked out the door. "What the hell you doing here?"

"Debbie called me," he said.

"Why the hell would Debbie call you?"

"I told her to."

"You told her to?" What, he had ESP or something? "You figure the sheriff needs some help?"

"Figure they do."

"They need a lawyer, not'n environmentalist."

"In Cloten, Karl, everyone needs an environmentalist."

The approach of the sheriff's car spared me a lecture. It

came up the street slow, looking for the right address—as if in Cloten you got to work very hard at that. I waved, and it pulled over, and a deputy got out. What, my law's not good enough for the sheriff, he's got to send a deputy? Didn't look old enough to be out of high school. Looked like he was playing cops.

"This the place with the event?" he asked.

"Not here," I said. "There. The sheriff coming?"

"Any reason for him to?"

"I voted for him."

The deputy stared. "Karl thinks we live in a democracy," Hardell said.

"Which one of you's the witness?"

"We do live in a democracy," I said.

"He is." Hardell pointed.

"You saw this goat being killed? That's why I'm here, right?"

"Saw it dead. Heard it being killed."

"Just heard?"

"I've heard it before. I'm not likely to confuse it with a lawn mower that won't start. You go over there, you're going to find that old boy with a dead goat up on a couple saw-horses."

"All right." The deputy looked pretty doubtful. "I'll check it out."

He walked across the lawn. Hardell followed. I was damned if I'd let Hardell interfere and not me, so I followed too. The deputy knocked on the door and watched it like it was going to jump him. Then he rang the doorbell. Finally the door opened and there was the teenage kid looking out at us, more sullen at ground level than from above. He looked past the deputy giving his speech about a complaint and said, "Har Dell," like it was two words, with a space between them. The deputy stopped, and the kid asked: "Are we in trouble?"

"Maybe, Lon," Hardell said. "Is your grandfather in?"

Of course his grandfather was in. Hadn't I just seen him over the fence? And how the hell did Hardell and the kid know each other, and where'd the kid learn to speak English like that, like he was showing he could pronounce it better than someone who come by it natural?

"The goat?" the kid asked.

"Yeah."

"I tried to tell him," the kid said. He stood in the door, the room a dark space behind him, and the smell of ginger and other strange spices coming out and mixing with the smell of corn tasseling, and 2-4-D from Eddie Jasper's Hi-Boy spraying outfit running in the field just behind my house. I was too familiar with the kid's expression—the same one Karl Junior used to have when he'd come home late and I was up waiting for him and he didn't know whether to be rebellious or sorry.

"You're admitting you broke a law?" the deputy asked.

"He's admitting nothing," Hardell said.

The deputy squinted at Hardell, standing there in loafers and black socks and shorts, legs as skinny as a leghorn rooster's. "You a lawyer?"

"He's an environmentalist," I said.

"One a them," the deputy said. He turned back to the kid. "You ought to cooperate," he said. "The best thing's to cooperate."

"Jesus," Hardell muttered to me. "What's this, Barney Fife?"

The kid moved back from the door, and the deputy stepped inside. The kid said: "Har Dell. You come too." I just followed along. When I stepped through the door after Hardell, the kid said: "Thank you."

"What?" I asked.

"Thank you, Mr. Karl Wagner, our neighbor," he said, "for finding an opportunity to visit."

What was I supposed to make of that? He sounded serious as hell. "You're welcome," I said. Then I thought he had to be sarcastic. Just like a teenager. He was the one breaking the law, not me.

"This way," he said, and headed down the hallway, reminded me of a butler in an old movie, and us the dinner party. The deputy followed, but I grabbed Hardell's elbow.

"What's with this kid?" I muttered.

"What do you mean?" Hardell asked, like he was newborn yesterday.

"Is he a smart-ass or what?" I said. "And where'd he learn to speak English?"

"I know what you mean," Hardell said. "Nothing makes you madder than when they speak the language."

"So, where'd he learn it?"

"Refugee camps. The kids pick up language fast."

"How do you know this stuff? For that matter, how the hell you know the kid, what's-his-name?"

"Lon. I've been helping out."

"You ain't Lutheran, Hardell."

"Oops. I never thought of that." He started for the hallway, but I stopped him again.

"This kid," I said. "He got something against me?"

"Any reason he should?"

"Hell no. I ain't never had a thing to do with him or his family."

Hardell sucked his teeth. You ever seen an old guy in loafers and shorts trying to look thoughtful? You could sell tickets.

"Well," he finally said, "seems he couldn't have anything against you then, right?"

"Right. Maybe he's just inscrutable."

"Could be."

"I don't know, though. Seems like he might be a smart-ass."

"Teenagers today."

That was a subject I could've warmed up to, but Hardell set off down the hall. We came out the back door, and sure enough, there was the evidence, couldn't be much plainer than that, and the old guy standing right next to it. Even if the deputy was blind and a moron, he'd be able to see what was going on.

"There," I said to Hardell as we walked across the dust that shoulda been a lawn. "You see?"

"I never doubted you, Karl."

The kid was saying something to his grandfather, a bunch of sounds I don't see how anybody understood it, and the old guy was listening like he could make a living at it, and then I heard my name, "Karl Wagner," like the kid was speaking up a wind and all of a sudden the wind stopped so my name could sit there by itself, and then the wind started in again, and both of them turned and looked at me.

"What are they saying about me?" I asked.

"Don't know," Hardell replied. "Couldn't hardly be bad, though, could it?"

The way they looked at me, though, made me feel like I was the criminal here. And the foreigner. Like I walked through their house and come out in the Twilight Zone, half-expected to see Rod Serling standing in the corner. There're still times when I wish Geraldine was around, and this was one of them. She had a way of roping the world in.

All those eyes looking at me—even the dead goat's on the plywood—like something was wrong with me. I used to sometimes feel the same way when Karl Junior and I'd have a big battle, and he'd finally go stomping off and leave me alone. The whole house'd be silent, like a big empty bell and me the clapper inside it, hanging there. Or the last time Katy and Sam were down with their parents, and things seemed to be going pretty well, until I let the kids get dirty and Sandy came back and had her snit. I'd been thinking of seeing if I could take the kids fishing the next day, but they all up and left, Karl Junior not saying a word to me, and there I was, listening to a crop-dusting plane in the distance while the kids waved me good-bye.

Now even the deputy was looking at me like I was to blame for something. Though maybe he just didn't have much use for anybody who wasn't breaking the law. It was the old guy stopped staring first. Like he hadn't been staring at all, only waiting for me to get closer. His face suddenly shattered—the ugliest smile I ever seen. Big, crooked yellow teeth going everywhere but straight, and wrinkles looking like an invasion. His eyes disappeared. Geraldine was always after me for being suspicious of people, but even I knew no one could smile that ugly and be insincere.

"Har Dell," he said, like the kid did, but even more two words, like he was slicing them off with that knife. Then he said, "Karl," the same way. I don't know how he did it, made it sound like it had four syllables.

Then he bent at the waist, keeping his legs straight. It took me a second to realize he was bowing, like when I'd watched him kill the goat. It was the strangest little thing I'd ever seen, like he'd been practicing it for a long time but didn't think he had it quite right, so he was still working on perfecting it. Then he came back up, and Hardell tried to do the same thing. What kind of idiot bows wearing shorts and loafers? If the old man bowed, then what Hardell did was something no language anywhere ever bothered to name. I was damned if I was going to make a fool of myself. So I put out my hand.

The whole thing made me forget we were here to arrest the old guy for breaking my law, and about the time I remembered, he was taking my hand and it was too late to jerk it back. He had a small hand, like a woman's. I didn't hardly know what to do with it, but all of a sudden he tightened his grip, tendons popped up, felt like they was cables. I firmed my own grip up quick.

He smiled away while we shook hands, and then said something to me.

"Grandfather says 'welcome,' " Lon said, surly as ever.

"Thanks," I said. "Welcome to him, too."

"Some welcome," the kid said.

"You better just translate, Lon," Hardell said. So the kid rattled off something, and the old guy smiled and nodded, and then we all stood there looking at each other.

"Does he know what's going on?" Hardell asked.

"I told him," Lon said.

"What'd he say?"

"Nothing. You came in."

That knocked me back a bit. The old guy'd just found out he was in trouble with the law, and Lon must've blamed me for it, and still he greets me like I'm a long-lost friend. Lon seemed to figure out what I was thinking. "Grandfather doesn't do things like I would," he said.

"That mean something?"

"It might." His speech was so perfect I couldn't tell if he was ticked off or not.

"Look," I said, "I ain't the one broke a law here."

"Neither had grandfather. Till you made up one for him to break."

I'll be damned if I'm going to have some teenager tell me my business. "Don't lay that on me," I said. "He didn't have to kill that goat."

People not taking blame for their own blame, that's something I can't stand. Karl Junior once wrecked the car and then blamed it on snowy roads. As if they snuck up on him. We had a hell of a fight on that one, not so much because he wrecked the car, but because he wouldn't admit he'd done it.

"This is going nowhere," Hardell said.

"Damn right it isn't."

The old man just watched.

"That law you got passed, Karl," Hardell said. "The big to-do about it. After that, kids at school started calling Lon 'Goat-Killer.' It's hard enough for him here, you know? So maybe you see why he's not real happy with you."

"Sorry, Lon," he said to the kid. "He just oughta know."

Lon tried to go on looking sullen, but the sullen was kind of stuck on his face now, not really part of it. One of these papier-mâché masks, peeling off in rain. Hell. I wished I was back in my house watching *Petticoat Junction*.

"I didn't mean for nothing like that to happen," I said.

"We know that," Hardell said. Suddenly he's a "we."

"I don't care what they call me," Lon said.

But he wasn't fooling anybody.

Then out of the blue the old guy started talking, looking at me like I understood, his hands carving triangles and circles in the air like he was chiseling words there to be sure they made sense to me. Not just waving his hands around but like he'd practiced this the way he'd practiced the bowing, and did it right. When he was done, he looked at me like I was supposed to answer some question.

Then he said something to Lon, and Lon said something back. But his grandfather wasn't going for it. He pointed at me and said something pretty sharp, and there wasn't much doubt about whether Lon was going to do what he wanted.

Lon made a face.

"He says you've come about the goat," he said. "He knows there's a law against it—*I* told him that—but he says what's the use of having a goat if you can't butcher it, and why would Americans make a law to keep people from eating what they've raised? So there must be a mistake in the law, and he'd like you to find where, since he doesn't understand."

The deputy looked at us, waiting for a chance to pounce back in and take charge like he thought he should. Hardell didn't say anything, just sucked his teeth.

Why was it suddenly my job to make sense of the law for

them? "Where are your parents?" I asked Lon. "Can't they explain this to him?"

"Working."

"Both of them?"

"Of course."

I don't know why everyone thinks they got to both work these days. That's half the trouble with kids, no one around to discipline them.

"So why don't they explain this to him?"

"He wants you to."

Again I couldn't tell if Lon was being a smart-ass or not. Inscrutable. "Where do they work?"

"The turkey factory."

"The Lutherans got them jobs at the Clear River turkey factory?" I asked Hardell.

"Better than a refugee camp."

"Not much."

Then I saw the kid's face. It'd got twisted up, trying to keep itself sullen but not doing well, and I realized that Hardell and me probably shouldn't be talking about his parents and their jobs that way. But the turkey factory—the place almost shut down a few years back because no one'd work there, butchering turkeys all day long, till they started bringing in some Mexicans and then, well, refugees. Some future. Come to America to work in the Clear River turkey plant, cutting off turkey heads all day.

"Hell," I said, "let's just forget it. Tell your grandfather he's right. There's a mistake. We'll just go home and pretend this never happened."

"Can't do that."

The deputy'd found his opening.

"What do you mean?"

"A law's been broken. I can't just forget it."

"Sure you can. It's my law. And I say forget it."

"It's the town's law. And it's my job to enforce it."

"You mean you're going to arrest this guy for doing something I don't care about now? You wouldn't even know about it if I hadn't called."

Now the deputy looked sullen.

"Well," Hardell said, "no one actually saw a crime being committed, right? Karl's your only witness, and he only heard, and it could've been, what was it you said, Karl?—a lawn mower that wouldn't start?"

I looked at the lawn that the goats'd eaten down to nothing, and then at the goat on the plywood, not likely to get up and start eating any more grass, and I thought there was some truth to Hardell's statement.

"Yeah," I said. "That was most likely it."

"Sure," the deputy said. "But there's a dead goat right there."

We all looked at the goat then, its bulging eyes, its neck open like a split radiator hose, its dirty white hair hanging in tangled strings, a few flies buzzing around it.

"Circumstantial," Hardell said. "Could've come from the Red Owl. Or the locker plant. Lon, you live here. Where you think that goat came from?"

I thought for a moment Lon was going to ask his grandfather, but he thought better of it. The old guy would've been too honest for his own good. Lon shrugged. "The locker plant, I guess."

"Can't do much with that," Hardell told the deputy.

"You sure you ain't a lawyer?" The deputy glared at Hardell.

"Just an environmentalist."

"Just as bad." The deputy adjusted his cap and walked across the dust. "Waste a my time," he called back before he disappeared. "Waste a the taxpayers' money."

Lon babbled at his grandfather, explaining what'd just happened. The old guy walked up to me and stuck out his hand and said something.

"He says 'thank you,'" Lon said. Then he hesitated. "Cousin."

"Cousin?"

Lon shrugged. "Neighbor. Something like. It's hard to translate."

"You're welcome," I said.

Lon translated, and when we were done shaking hands, I bowed, figuring why not, what could it hurt, and the old man bowed back, and then Hardell bowed, and we all kind of bobbed around for a bit.

"Course, Karl," Hardell said, "you realize that since they didn't kill a goat here, you're going to have to listen to them not doing it again, probably."

I'd forgotten that.

"Lon," I said, "ask your grandfather why's he bother to raise these goats at all? Why not just be done with the whole thing?"

The old guy nodded as Lon spoke, and then he spoke to me quietly. Like he didn't know we spoke two different languages.

"He says," Lon said, "what else would he do? Sit in a big, square house and wait to die? He says the family is gone all day and he sees the . . . trouble—that's not quite the right word—in their eyes when they come home. He doesn't want them to see more trouble when they look at him. And raising goats helps him like living here a little more."

I couldn't say much to that.

"Trouble is," Hardell said finally, "pretty soon someone else is going to complain."

"He could butcher out of town," I said. "I bet Ed Olsen'd let him work out there—he's crazy enough to allow most anything. Or Steele Hendrickson, now that he's recovered from whatever it was got into him. Might even like the company."

"I could work on that," Hardell said. "Course he'd need a pickup. You got one, don't you, Karl?"

"Yes I do," I said. But I didn't promise anything. I'd met my neighbors, and as Geraldine would say, they were people just like me. Still, I couldn't quite see myself chasing goats into my pickup and driving out to Ed Olsen's with them in the back, and Lon's grandfather beside me, him talking one language and me another, and the cornfields out the window same as ever. Still, maybe I'd lend them my pickup, and Hardell could do the driving and chasing, seeing how he thrives on that kind of thing.

When we left, everyone seemed in a pretty good mood. Even Lon wasn't looking sullen. His grandfather offered to share goat meat with us, but not even Hardell accepted the offer. When I got back home, the TV was still on. Jackie Gleason was doing his bragging routine on *The Honeymooners*. I watched for a bit, but he was just going to get shown for a fool again. I hit the remote, and the house was mighty silent.

Then I noticed a klunking sound outside. I climbed the

steps and looked out the window, standing back from the glass. He was down there again, working away, the plywood knocking against the sawhorses. He had the goat quartered, and was talking and gesturing with the knife, and Lon was watching, learning something that'd never do him a damn bit of good, and I could see he knew it, the way he stood first on one leg and then the other, swatting at flies.

Lon looked up at the window once, and I thought for a second he saw me. I almost waved, but his grandfather said something, and he looked down again. He couldn't have seen me anyway. I took a step closer to the glass to prove it, but he didn't look up again. Pretty soon he and his grandfather shuffled across the dust into their house, carrying meat.

I looked down at the empty yard, dry as a desert. In one corner two goats grazed on a few tufts of sad grass. Beyond them, Eddie Jasper swung his Hi-Boy around at the end of the round, the booms making a big arc, dripping spray. It seemed those goats knew all about the goat that was gone and didn't see any sense in eating grass but did it anyway, just because they were goats. Their jaws moved up and down. They ate among the flies. I got to wishing Karl Junior and me got along better and that he hadn't moved to Minneapolis and that he'd bring the kids down more often.

That made me remember the boat I'd bought before I retired, thinking I'd more or less live on the river once I left the farm. I never used it much, though—hadn't even thought of it after Geraldine died until last year, when I had the grandkids and I thought of taking them out, before Sandy and Karl Junior decided to be upset and leave early. The kids'd love it—with Spam sandwiches and Coke, going down to the river around ten some summer night and getting in the boat, and the river coming smooth and dark around the bends, and pulling big catfish out of the water into the light of a Coleman.

How long I stood there, I don't know. It was the streetlight across the way coming on that made me realize it was getting dark outside, and people'd be able to see me through the window. The Hi-Boy'd gone from the fields. I backed away and went downstairs and stood by the phone for a while, thinking how to say it all.

But even if I got it said, I knew what Karl Junior'd say, how the kids had their own lives, baseball practice and games in the summer, things that couldn't be missed. And Sandy'd probably complain that she'd been reading how the Minnesota River is polluted from all the runoff from feedlots, something like that, and she didn't want the kids on it.

In a few minutes *Green Acres* would be on. Arnold the pig was always good for a few laughs, and after that, *Hogan's Heroes* would almost get me to bed. I thought of Lon and his grandfather in their house together. Those goats across the way were standing in the dark, eating grass because they were goats. I sat down—I'd lost the heart to stand—and stared at the phone and kind of wished Hardell'd come back. Hogan's never going to get away from Klink even if he is smarter, and anyway, I've seen it. But I knew how Karl Junior'd sound when he heard it was me on the line. Polite and a bit too friendly, and waiting to see why I'd called. Like there had to be a reason, like I was a policeman or something.

Bird Shadows

Y OU never lose the clay from off your heels. Born a hick, you are a hick for life. The pull of land is like a black, black tide, a strong black moon over thick black water, water so thick one walks upon it and carries it forever upon one's heels, water like a glue. It's a tide that ebbs and flows in the corpuscles of the blood, in the darkness of the gut and the compressing caverns of the heart. One can make it ebb and ebb and ebb until it has seemed to ebb to dryness, an ocean withdrawing into itself. But one can never drain it dry.

I used to listen to my own heart tick against the pillow, the pulse in my ear rustle on the linen, and I would fall asleep thinking I knew what tide was strongest in my blood. If Sheila was beside me, I was sure of it. What I didn't know was that my father was a dam and that beyond him, the tide of land still roared, black and thick as ever. He died. The tide rushed toward me. "Come back," my mother said, "for a year, no more, to help me." And my lemming heart ticked yes.

❧

My daughter picks at her food. She sits across from me and moves the pasta shells around in her marinara sauce. She stares at the garlic bread, takes desultory bites. I wish she'd eat more. It would be good to see her enjoy what I've prepared for her.

But she doesn't eat. She's been divorced three times. After this last time, she showed up here. When I got in from the fields, she'd already moved her things into her old room. I knocked the dirt off my boots and walked into the house. I could feel the difference. The house contained breathing other than mine. It contained her—my line. It had reached for her and now it held her.

"Eat," I say. "It's good food." I tap my fork in the air in the direction of her plate.

She sets her fork down. She has only one thing on her mind. "Don't sell the farm, Dad," she says. "Promise me you won't sell the farm."

I cut a shell with the edge of my fork, stab it, lift it to my mouth. I really am a decent cook. I wish she'd enjoy it more.

❧

As a boy, I fed the chickens barefoot because I liked the way the fresh manure, mottled white and brown, squeezed up between my toes. You never lose the shit from off your heels. You may, as I did, think you've escaped, you may fool others, may even fool yourself. But on your heels and in your heart the hick remains, though you hate that hick and spend your youth and love to purge it. Experience is a mask, not a cure. The land clings in your blood. My neighbors go about their chores and duties ignorant, never knowing. They think me misanthropic, and I am. I stay within my fences, succumbing to this land I never wanted to inherit, like a slow bear no longer even pacing behind its bars.

For a long time, though, I thought that only men could be hicks. I thought that women washed the tide out of their bodies with their blood, that month by month they purged themselves in a cleansing more direct than anything men have. And this, I thought, was why the land and house had captured only men, leaving it to them, by force or guile, to capture women who would provide the men that the house and land would capture.

But here my daughter is, in this house that is her house as much as mine, as it was my father's: an ordering of timber that has funneled generations like drops of amber through a narrow, wooden neck. It's strange to see her here, not wife or daughter-in-law, but progeny itself, female, with full chest and tight, blue-jeaned crotch and uncorded neck and tapered fingers, strange to see all this in the low-ceilinged rooms, moving with soft step and breath over old linoleum.

Sheila loved the cormorants. On wooden pier posts, on webbed feet, they would stand and spread their wings. To catch the sun, she told me. When they dove into the water, they plunged right through their shadows, the hooked beak first, then the rest of the black body. Underwater, flickering, they became their shadows, darker than the ones they dove into. Sheila and I would stand, tossing canned sardines to them. I held her around the waist and felt her laughter through my hand.

☙

My daughter tells me: "I want the farm."

She's carrying a five-gallon pail of feed into the farrowing house. A man would let the pail swing down from his shoulder, and brace his elbow just enough against his hip to keep the pail from knocking against his knee. She, however, leans far over against the weight of the pail, far to the left, and her arm goes out around the curve of her hip, and the pail bangs against her knee. It makes her limp. But she carries it. The sows grunt and snort when she lifts it over the gates.

"Don't overfeed them," I warn her. I know she won't, but I say it anyway.

She dumps the feed into the trough in quick, angry motions. I go back outside. She comes out of the dim doorway with the empty pail and drops it on the ground. Feed dust clings to her hair, and a yellow streak of it fades her cheek.

The pail rings against the ground, tips over and rolls a little way, the wire handle clanking. "I don't want the money," she says. "I don't care what kind of price you can get for it. I want the house. I want the land."

I look at the sky. "Looks like rain, maybe," I say. "Probably better not cut hay. Suppose we ought to castrate those pigs today."

"Goddamnit, Dad!" She comes toward me, then turns and kicks the pail. It booms, flies through the air, hits the farrowing house, booms again. The entire farrowing house shakes as every startled sow in there bangs against its gate. It's as if the farrowing house itself grunts and squeals. I hope none of the sows crushed a baby pig.

"You're not listening to a goddamn word I say!"

"I'm listening," I tell her. "You want the land and house. Now, we got to get those pigs castrated."

I head up to the shop to get the razor blades. I look up at the old house. It's waiting. Like always. Behind me, I can hear her limping. She kicked that pail mighty hard. I almost turn and go to her, to wipe the dust from her cheek, then take off her boot and hold her foot in both my hands. But I look up at the house and keep on walking.

Sheila was with me when my mother called. She was reading on the couch. She sat with both feet tucked far under her, like a cat would sit if it had only two legs. She went on reading through the phone call. I must have given little enough away, because when I hung up the phone, she finished the paragraph she was reading before looking up.

"What's going on?" she asked.

"Dad died."

"Oh, Rafe!" She came to me. Tears glistened in her eyes. She pressed herself to me, stroked my hair.

Her tears made my own cheeks wet.

"I'll need to go back to Cloten. For a while. Until things are straightened out."

She kissed me, her arms tight around me.

"I'll have to take a train tomorrow. But it shouldn't be long. A few months, maybe."

She nodded.

"Of course," she said. "Of course you have to go, Rafe." Her hair brushed my face.

Neither of us knew it then, but I'd already lost her. Had I known the future, I would have wept myself.

My daughter has tied her hair back with a rubber band to keep it from getting in her way. She holds a baby pig upside down by its hind legs, its underside facing away from her, toward me. The pig arches, tries to bite her leg. With her knee she pushes it away, keeping her hold firm.

I splash iodine between the legs, then make the slits. There's a little blood. I pull out the nuts and cut the cords. The pig squeals and tries to bite her again. She stays firm, pushing it away. I splash more iodine onto the empty skin, then nod. She sets the pig down. It runs a short distance, stops and rubs its rear end in the straw.

Suddenly she grabs the knife from me. "You hold," she says. She inserts a new razor blade, splashes some iodine on it, and waits. She expects resistance, maybe, but I don't pause. I just grab a pig and hold it for her.

She does well. Presses a little hard with the blade, maybe. It's just a touch you need. But she doesn't hesitate in any of it. If it's bothering her, she doesn't let it show. Her hands, like mine, end up bloody and stained.

She won't give up the blade. For the rest of the morning, I hold and she cuts. She learns the touch, the lightness of it. But it doesn't matter. She doesn't know it, but there's nothing at all she needs to prove to me. She just thinks there is.

❧

No one falls off silos. Of the high things on the plains that one might fall off of, grain elevators being built, with men on scaffolds, are the only ones that claim victims. Silos, on the other hand, look dangerous, but men climb them up and down with the same nonchalance with which a squirrel hangs facedown on a tree. Every boy, before he reaches adolescence, climbs the silo, sits on the smooth tin roof curving under him. Mothers worry, but no one stops him. If he's ready, he's safe. It's a rite of passage. No one falls off silos.

I said none of this to Sheila. Or to my mother. I stared into the past when I should have stared into the future. Sheila's hand was on my neck, and she pulled my face down to her shoulder, expecting me to weep. But I shut my eyes and pictured the setting sun behind the grove, the shadows of the trees already stretched out along the fields, lengthening toward the grassy fence lines. Above the shadows, in orange light, I pictured my father standing. Given to drama, and no doubt slightly drunk, he had his arms outstretched. Far out on the field, the shadow of the silo, long and phallic, was topped by a thin, extended figure. It might have been the shadow of a great and ancient bird.

High up, swallows flicker by him. Were the day stormy, they would be lower, the insects pressed downward by the heavy air. But he's chosen a fair day. He waits to catch his breath. The climb up is a hard one. While he breathes, his white hair, burned orange, wavers like a halo around his head. Then he arcs off the curving roof, off and out, his arms still spread. The shadow of the ancient bird flickers with incredible speed over furrow and fence line, leaps the house, covers a mile in a couple of seconds, disappears into the shadows of the grove, and meets my father with a sodden thud as he meets the ground.

Sheila kissed me again. I couldn't respond. I could only think of the lie my father let my mother believe. I should have let the past go, let him go, let it all go, and looked to the future. Then I might have suspected this would be one of the last kisses she would ever give me, and not let the future happen.

Instead, the shadow of an evil, deformed bird, with bent bones and diving flight, hung over the room, and I didn't even feel her lips.

At the supper table my daughter eats a little better. The work's made her hungry. Or she's showing that it hasn't ruined her appetite. I've cooked chicken in a curry sauce—a small memory; I cooked the same thing for Sheila just the day before my mother called that time. Sheila and I spent all afternoon cooking, laughing, eating. After my wife died—she cooked meat and potatoes, decent food but only that—I started cooking again, different foods. I have to shop in Clear River to find what I need. Since I returned to Cloten, no one until my daughter had shared a meal like this with me. I watch her eat.

She says nothing during the meal, nothing about the farm. We talk of other things, awkward with each other. The words we aren't saying lie between us. I'd rather it weren't so, but I see no way out of it. After supper, with coffee, I tell her:

"BigJim Anderson's coming over tomorrow."

I've been dreading it, but one has to follow through. She looks at me with real venom in her eyes. When she speaks, it's in her voice too.

"Bastard," she says.

If this land hadn't already congealed my heart, she'd fracture it. To be called a bastard by your own daughter. I can't look at her. I'm too ashamed for both of us.

"You don't give a shit, do you?" she goes on. "You'll sell. You don't give a shit about me at all."

She's spilled some coffee on her blue jeans, and she says, "Damn," and goes behind me. Her cup crashes in the sink, and silverware clangs. When the sound fades, I hear swallows outside, chirping in the dusk. They rise and fall as the night settles.

"I care about you."

It's the first time I've been weak since she arrived. It opens up a dangerous longing, to go to her and hug her and give her what she wants. The house is waiting. The land is waiting, stretched out on itself. To see what I will do.

I wait back. One can learn lessons from one's captor. Mistakes can be corrected if they're minor. She comes around and sits on the table.

"You have a funny way of showing it."

One stockinged foot is swinging, the one that kicked the pail. I resist again the urge to hold it, to caress the bruise away.

"I hurt you and Mom," she goes on. "I know that. I made a mess of my life. But I've learned. I'm sorry for all that."

It's hard to let her think I'm punishing her for old mistakes. It's hard to hear a daughter plead. My only child, to hear her plead. She waits for me to answer. When I don't, she says, "I can do it, Dad. I can run this place. Didn't I do good work today?"

Of course she did good work. It's not easy, not to tell her so. We both wait, with the house. Of the three of us, she has the least resistance. She speaks again: "I've got nothing, Dad. I've screwed up everything I've tried. Marriage and jobs and everything."

She's almost crying now. "I don't have anything. Except this farm and house. And you."

And me. She's telling me I'm one of the few things she has. But if I reach out to her now, everything goes on. On and on. The house is making sounds, creaking in the wind, sighing in the air moving through it. I dare not look at her.

"You're getting old, Dad," she says. Real quiet. "What'll I have once you're gone? And I love this place. I love the land. I never knew it, but I do. I should have never left."

She loves it. What can I say to that? She's been elsewhere, and she loves this. But I never told my mother that no one falls off silos. I let her believe what comforted her. And I never told my daughter—how could I?—about Sheila. What would I say now?

"Anderson's coming over," I say. "I better do the dishes."

I get up, and she stares at me in disbelief, then rushes from the house. The door slams so hard the glass breaks and spews over the linoleum, sparkling in the twilight. When I pick it up, it cuts me.

Months turned into more months. He'd made a mess of things. The fields had gone to weed, the machinery to rust and rot. He'd run up bills and never paid them, and had lost credit at nearly every place in Cloten and Clear River. Three weeks after the funeral, when I had a pretty good picture of the state of things, I told my mother: "Sell the place. Sell it all. Get what you can and pay the bills, and use what's left over for a house in town."

"Rafe!" she said, astonished—and ashamed, too, I think, that I would care so little. "I can't do that! Your father put everything he had into this farm."

I could have made things clear. The words were on my tongue: *he jumped, Mom. He wasn't working. He didn't slip. He jumped. He didn't put everything he had into this farm. It's just he didn't have much, and it* took *what he had.*

Instead, I let her believe. I shut the account books and gazed at their ragged covers. How do you tell your mother her illusion isn't yours?

I didn't know I was trapping myself. Letting her live her illusion, I forced myself to help her live it. It took me years to find this out. Too late to do me good. But not my daughter. Perhaps not her.

❀

I do the dishes. The water turns pink from the cut in my hand, but there's no sense in bandaging it until I'm done. The soap at least should cleanse the wound.

She comes in as it's getting dark. I'm reading, by a single bulb. She sits down in the shadows of the couch, watches me for a while.

"You cut yourself," she notes.

I nod. "The glass did."

"I'm sorry. I'll buy a new pane."

"It doesn't matter."

Maybe she understands what I mean. She doesn't reply. I ask, finally: "Where've you been?"

"On top of the silo. I watched the sunset. The land's green, and then it turns orange from up there. This orange light that tinges everything. It's so beautiful, Dad. Do you ever see it anymore?"

My ears roar. The land is pulsing, flowing in them. It's all I can hear.

Then, over the pounding, she says, "You don't think a woman could be a farmer, do you? You don't think I could handle it."

"You'd be a good farmer," I say.

My second weakness. The whole land is flowing in the room. It's rushing in my ears and veins, hurrying me along, urging me to speak even as it drowns me—urging me to give in, to dive beneath the hard, black surface and let my life disappear for good.

She's waiting for an explanation. I don't know how I manage not to give one.

"It's getting late," I say. "I've got to go to bed."

The land held me, through my mother's foolish illusion, until it could grip me itself, until it had worn me down with hours and demands. Until I lost my one resistance. I fought it with long letters, my eyes burning at midnight after wearing myself out with constant work all day. I tried to maintain that other tide of heart. I apologized, told Sheila I'd be back, that I just had to straighten things out so that my mother wouldn't lose everything. She wrote back. Twice a week we wrote. The farm gave me no time for travel. No time for anything but it.

I'd told her a couple of months. After six, she asked me when I would return. A few more months, I said. Then in almost every letter she began to ask. I should have heard the plea. If I had, I might still have broken free, fought the black, soily current sucking at my shoulders.

Then it came, after almost a year and a half—the phone call I should have anticipated. I knew with sickening certainty I'd made a huge mistake. The land and house were revenging themselves on my dreams of breaking free. I should have married Sheila and brought her back, trapped and held her, given her to them.

I left weeds growing in the fields and took a plane to the coast and found her, the only love I've ever known, living with another man in the rooms and bed where we had lived and slept. I was like an intruder. I stood in those rooms a stranger, a stranger in my own life, a bystander. Sheila looked at me like someone drowned, and someone who was not me was touching her while I watched. Sheila. I reached out to her, but she could no longer save me. She looked at me like someone already gone, already swallowed and taken. Standing there on the shore of my life, I called out to her, but the land pulled me back, sucked me to the airport and sucked the plane through the dark sky to my future, to the woman I'd nearly drown beside—given by the land—but never learn to love, and to my mother's death and daughter's birth and me holding her and vowing that all of this would end, that I would give the land no sons, would drown no children in it, that with me would end this crushing tide.

Before I sleep, I feel my heartbeat slow. I feel death practicing within me. Tonight I don't sleep. The light leaves late. The sounds of birds fade and stop. Then my daughter's quiet feet are on the steps. She moves in her room, the floorboards creak and groan—sounds so familiar, so intense. Waves of memory lap me. She isn't sleeping either. We're lying, both awake, our doors open, and only dark between us. If I whispered, she'd hear me.

"Once you're gone," she'd said, "I'll have nothing." It's what I vowed to give her. My gift to her: her own life—not bound to this place or this house that took my father, took me, that sustained a lie, pulled me away from the life I meant to live, from the woman I meant to love.

My daughter doesn't want the gift. Doesn't even know it's a gift. Thinks it's a deprivation. I haven't felt so knotted up, so hard, since I stood in Sheila's room and saw another man living my life with her. Now here's my daughter, seeing me stealing her life as I saw that man steal mine. As I saw my father steal my future.

It's good to have her here. It's the first good thing I've known in this house for a long, long time. I think of how she's my daughter, the one I have, given through all that was taken from me. I lie quietly, listening for her breathing. The wind outside the house, moving through the eaves, across the shingles, hides her breathing. I could be alone here. I could be all alone.